The Leopard Sword

The Leopard Sword

MICHAEL CADNUM

VIKING

VIKING
Published by the Penguin Group
Penguin Putnam Books for Young Readers,
345 Hudson Street, New York, New York 10014, U.S.A.
Penguin Books Ltd, 80 Strand, London WC2R 0RL, England
Penguin Books Australia Ltd, Ringwood, Victoria, Australia
Penguin Books Canada Ltd, 10 Alcorn Avenue, Toronto, Ontario, Canada M4V 3B2
Penguin Books (N.Z.) Ltd, 182-190 Wairau Road, Auckland 10, New Zealand

Penguin Books Ltd, Registered Offices: Harmondsworth, Middlesex, England

Published in 2001 by Viking, a division of Penguin Putnam Books for Young Readers.

1 3 5 7 9 10 8 6 4 2

LIBRARY OF CONGRESS CATALOGING-IN-PUBLICATION DATA
Cadnum, Michael.
The leopard sword / Michael Cadnum
p. cm.
Summary: A knight's squire, exhausted from the Crusades, must use his sword
to fight attacking infidels during the return voyage to England.
ISBN 0-670-89908-9
[1. Knights and knighthood—Fiction. 2. Crusades—Third, 1189-1192—Fiction.
3. Middle Ages—Fiction.] I. Title.
PZ7.C11724 Le2002 [Fic]—dc21 2002018933

Printed in USA
Set in Bembo
Designed by Kelley McIntyre

for Sherina

◆

Tide so high
our boats part
the treetops

The Leopard Sword

ONE

The *San Raffaello* began her turn, her oars churning the water.

But then a wind off the sea came up, and small boats continued to gather nearby, impeding the oars—boats filled with camp followers and Templar knights, all crying farewells. The last load of war booty had been heaved up onto the deck from the tenders, and now servants gathered the chests and leather bags. Beyond, on the horizon, a line of Saracen war vessels blocked our route, and despite my private prayer I knew there would be a sea battle before night.

But as yet most of us gave the enemy no thought. We crowded the landward side of the galley, our eyes on the army camped along the shore of the Holy Land we were putting behind us, the Crusading force of King Richard Lionheart and the distant, half-hidden sulk of the Saracen tents. I stood beside my tall, brown-haired friend Edmund,

1

both of us leaning out over the ship's side so that we could gaze back at the gleam of afternoon sun on helmets and spear points, everything that we were leaving.

Nearly every capable fighting man in Christendom had joined in the effort to free Jerusalem from the grip of the Infidel armies, and that struggle was far from over. But we were a ship of wounded and disease-wracked knights and squires, our warring done. Many of us were not expected to live to see the Greek island of Chios, our first port of call on our long voyage back to England.

My master Sir Nigel raised his voice. "Hubert, it's a pleasure to taste salt after all that fly-dirt," he told me, strong feeling straining his voice as he turned away from the sight of the Crusading army, blinking tears.

I was quick to agree with him, but I knew his heart. "Seawater is a cure for our ills, my lord," I said in apparent agreement.

But a squire empties his master's chamber pot, when servants are sick or few, and a squire hears his knight cursing demons in his sleep. I knew Sir Nigel was brokenhearted at leaving the fighting. We had spent long weeks laying siege to the walled city of Acre, and had clashed with our enemy when the city fell, and later at the bloody battle at Arsuf. Loyalty and custom required our departure with our sick and war-battered companions. Sir Nigel cradled his heavily bandaged arms, unable to hide his tears, forced by his injuries to depart before Jerusalem could be won.

The captain sang out orders in Genoese as Sir Rannulf made his way through the battle gear and treasure on the deck, crutch-propped warriors and yelling ship's mates, calling through his scarred lips for Edmund. My friend was quick, joining his master and Edmund's own man Osbert, gathering together the goatskin bags of silver-chased scimitars and knives. As I hurried over the slatted vents in the wooden decking, I caught the odor of the rowers, a sharp, pungent whiff of sweat and human soil, and a waft of body heat.

I joined Edmund in securing our baggage, lashing it together, as a tall young squire called Nicholas de Foss asked, "Whose gear is this?" He indicated our equipment, hauberks and shields Edmund and I had fastened tidily together.

It was true that our gear occupied a central place on deck, but Sir Nigel and Sir Rannulf were knights of good name, and servants and mariners avoided it without complaint.

"It's in the way of every man here," said Nicholas. He was golden-haired and freckled, older than my own eighteen years and a good two handsbreadths taller. He spoke quietly, with an evenhanded disdain for me—something we often encountered from the Franks, but unusual from other Englishmen.

Then his master limped into view, a large man with a set frown, a square jaw, and a dazzling blue tunic, dark along the hem with long-dried gore. "Move all this," said the squire, in an even harsher voice, now that his master could hear, "so my master Sir Jean can walk the deck unhindered." He offered me the subtlest glance of apology as he spoke, performing his duty.

Jean de Chartres had toppled off his warhorse while drunk, and sprung a sinew in the days before the city of Acre had fallen. Sir Jean's leg had swollen so he could not fit it into his mail leggings, or force it into a stirrup. During the battle such sick and injured knights had been forced by their wounds to labor in the rear, their lances angled proudly but far from any living enemy. Rumor had it that Sir Jean had nearly killed a young washerwoman for spilling water on his poor share of war spoils—a worn carpet, a hard-used Saracen saddle, and a few worn coins. Men said he had beaten his previous, Frankish, squire with a mailed fist just before the battle's end.

Now Sir Jean listed from side to side as he walked, his jaw outthrust, a sack of wine seeping through its seams at his side. As the ship heaved upward and gently fell again, he nearly toppled, and Nicholas caught him to keep him upright.

"We'll all need our armor soon, Sir Jean," said Sir Nigel evenly.

Nigel carried one broken arm in the other, having fallen off his warhorse giving chase to a Saracen emir after the fierce battle. My master was a very different man from the knight who had set forth from England just a few months ago. His close-cropped hair was shot through with more silver than before, and despite all the pain he must have felt, he wore a look of solemn acceptance. Suffering can be a gift from Heaven, and Nigel never asked for pain-dulling poppy wine, although we had a clay bottle of it. His broken arms had been set and bound by a Templar surgeon, who pressed the medicine on us and told us to pray for the help of the Archangel Michael himself, patron saint of the injured.

"Those of us still willing to fight," Jean of Chartres was saying, "will enjoy the opportunity." Talk was that he had outstanding gambling debts in his homeland that few knights could afford. Nearly all his worldly treasure was in the slack, nearly empty purse at his belt.

I made a point of studying the seven Infidel galleys, embarrassed on behalf of the Chartrian knight. The Infidel ships were no longer so far away. Edmund and I had studied these menacing vessels from the shore, and Sir Nigel had explained that these particularly deadly ships were called *gallea sottile,* galleys built for ramming other ships.

"For men of courage like us, there is still blood to spill," continued Sir Jean in Norman French, emphasizing *courage* and *sangre* to anyone who would listen.

Many men had hoped to die in service to Our Lord, not because they hated life, but because the Church had promised that all those who fell in such battle would win Heaven. Sir Jean's tone was less belligerent now, as he fingered the yellow bird stitched onto the front of his tunic. A corner of the bird emblem—a swift, I thought—had come loose, and he tried to press it back into place.

I was thankful that I had buried the sprig of dried rue my mother had given me on a hilltop from which the Holy City could be seen. I would never set foot within the sacred walls, but I prayed I would live to see my family at the end of my travels—and not lose my life now, at the hands of Saracen seamen.

"There is no shortage of courage," Sir Nigel was reminding Sir Jean, "anywhere among us."

"The little squire here," said Nicholas, indicating me with a nod and something like a smile, "was the picture of courtesy just now, agreeing to shift these bags."

There are taller men, and there are shorter men. I nudged the sheathed sword lashed onto a trunk at my feet, secure with our other war gear. I knew too well what it was like to cut flesh with a sharp edge, but just then I was willing to do it once again.

The two knights eyed each other. "I have taught him knightly patience," said Sir Nigel. "But he's the son of a prayerful woolman, and he learned fast."

"How wise of him," said Sir Jean.

If an enemy had not been available in the distance, all of us would have found reason to fall upon each other.

But our vessel gained momentum, and even the shrillest-voiced servant fell silent as we craned necks and half climbed the hot-board—the freeboard planks that kept waves from washing the deck—to watch the enemy ships ahead of us, no longer so far away.

One voice in a London accent lifted high in a fervent Our Father, the holy Latin silencing and shaming what had been the bitter squabbling among us, none of us happy to be leaving the Crusade. The prayer done, Sir Nigel knelt to our bundled equipment, and with his weak and injured arms tried to undo the knots.

"Outfit me in my armor," said Sir Nigel, as I knelt to help him, "and buckle on my sword."

All around us came the sounds of jingling mail and creaking leather, and the low, rhythmic chime of whetstones against blades.

TWO

A Christian ship, tacking hard and leaving a wide wake, was driving west far ahead of us. Even though the Saracen galleys closed fast, I told myself that the enemy vessels would be no match for the *Sint Markt,* a sturdy Low Country freighter.

The ship and the galleys were like designs in a tapestry— the golden sail, the wide blade of the rudder, the gleaming rise and fall of enemy oars. As I watched, the vessels seemed to move deliberately, the sailing ship working merrily against the breeze, the Saracens gliding soundlessly, as though it were all sport, and nothing harmful could follow.

I tried briefly to spy Edmund and to catch his eye, but I could see him nowhere in the throng of knights and squires now crowded forward to watch the distant Crusader ship. The *Sint Markt,* her sail fluttering, made a last-moment maneuver as we looked on, turning herself before the onrushing galley, heading into her attacker prow forward.

I once believed I knew something of war. My father's house had been graced with kind and cheerful servants, and during my boyhood, teachers explained to me which stars in the nightly dome were Taurus, and which Orion the hunter, lifting his weapon to strike a blow. I played at war with my sister Mary, who joined in eagerly—we arranged our hearth-knights made of straw in wide battle formations. On a sunny afternoon we would be taken down to the millpond and allowed to row in coblets, small craft designed for children. I knew how hard it was, even in play, to take a boat's impact in the side of a vessel, and how the wily boater will turn prow forward, to give the assaulting craft a smaller target, one less likely to capsize.

But now that I had tasted war, I felt I knew nothing about battle, or, in truth, about much else. The massacre of two thousand prisoners, at King Richard's command, had made me believe that war was a butcher's craft, and not a knight's. I had taken a man's life in the recent battle, with Heaven's blessing, but I hoped it would be many a long season before I would see fighting again.

Now the onrushing Infidel galley had two bronze battering rams thrust forward like horns. The gray prow of the Flemish vessel wedged violently between these rams, and yet even when white wood and jagged gaps appeared along the Crusader ship's wales, I believed the damage was slight. I thought the sailing ship would master the long, slender attacking craft as the enemy galley backed away, and then drew alongside the larger ship. The swarming bodies of Saracen swordsmen streamed into the broad-beamed freighter, an attack we could hear even at our distance, the shrill of voices, and the unsettling ring of iron on steel.

Aboard our ship, anguished voices were raised at the sight of faraway Crusaders raising shields, parrying blows, sunlight glinting off mail-clad bodies. Many of the far-off knights clambered onto the castles, the wooden structures prominent on the ship's stern and bow, but even as they beat off the flood of boarders, another Saracen *gallea* approached from the opposite side, and every voice onboard our ship was raised in protest, a ragged roar as we sought the intervention of Heaven.

In a deliberate, pretty maneuver the second galley hooked the side of the Crusader ship and opened a long, ugly rent, splinters of wood flying. The prow of this second attacker locked firmly in the Flemish ship's ribs. This meant that the Saracens had to flow over a single point near the galley's prow, and the flashing blades of two or three brave knights showed that this foray was being held off, and our voices lifted in an encouraging cheer.

We were no longer so distant from the fighting. The time between the flash of a far-off weapon and the sound of the blow, blade against armor, was less and less as the power of our oarsmen propelled us closer in sweeping strokes. The remaining enemy galleys turned, aiming their prows in our direction. At a shouted command from the captain, our galley took a wide turn, leaving an arcing wake in the water.

The *San Raffaello*'s captain was a tanned, bald-headed man with a short white beard and muscular forearms. He climbed the stern castle, briefly shielded his eyes, and descended again, barking further commands. Eager as our knights and squires might be to join the fight, our voices lost some of their strength as we measured our own galley against the enemy's longer, sleeker warships, each armed with a pair of waterline rams.

The *Sint Markt* foundered as we left her behind, canting so severely to one side that she forced the prow of one of the attacking galleys downward. Bright oars streamed water, working powerlessly, the ship a helpless, many-legged insect.

Just then Edmund appeared, carrying a large wooden chest, an enormous cask, fitted with leather and green brass hinges. Osbert, Edmund's new manservant, made a show of helping with this load, but he did little more than flutter. My friend set down the chest, and Osbert tried to shift it into a new position, failing to move it an inch. We worked to stow as much of our treasure as we could in the confines of this chest, and then Edmund carried it below for safety.

The *Sint Markt* was settling into the water behind us now, and some of our men cried out in futile protest, and many prayed in various tongues—Burgundian, Norman, Saxon— all beseeching Our Lady. Two knights remonstrated with our captain, forced to speak in an easy-to-understand pan-tomime: *Turn the ship around,* pointing, making the sign of the cross, and other, harsher gestures: *They are killing Christians.*

"We must help them," said Edmund quietly.

Enemy galleys were gaining on us.

"How should we help that shipload of fighting men, Edmund?" asked Sir Nigel. "What do you suggest that we do?"

Edmund lowered his gaze, and I could see him formulating tactics, imagining hand-to-hand combat. He looked to me and I spoke up for both of us, to spare Edmund the embarrassment of confessing an ignorance we both shared. "You will have to teach us the keener points of sea war, my lord."

"We'll have a battle of our own soon enough," said Sir Nigel. "You'll learn—we'll send a shipload of Saracens to the devil."

As much as I admired Sir Nigel, and prayed for his recovery, sometimes his view of upcoming combat surprised me. I knew he was a man of feeling, his moods changing hour by hour, and I knew he was a worshipful man in his way, whispering prayers each night before he slept. But I had seen sling stones punch the earth at his feet as he criticized the enemy's marksmanship and did nothing to seek a hiding place.

"Lash the sword into my hand," he was saying, in the same tone of voice in which he would have ordered another cup of wine.

I did as I was commanded, although I knew each knot caused him agony, until the broadsword was tied into his grip. I prayed that no fighting would be necessary, that fatigue would weaken the Saracen oarsmen. And I understood that my master wanted to die fighting, sword in hand, rather than return to England a crippled warrior.

Two long, sleek galleys, each swifter and narrower than the *San Raffaello*, shot along on either side of us now, water rushing under our keel. Our own men were well advanced in breaking out helmets, shaking sword belts free of entanglements, arms working into the chain mail mittens many knights wore instead of gauntlets.

Sir Rannulf approached us, already garbed in mail, his sword at his side. The battle had drained Sir Rannulf, and for many days he had been leaning on a staff. Now the weary knight he had been was suddenly gone, replaced by a man eager once again to test an enemy.

"They carry hooked pikes and halberds," said Rannulf through his scarred lips. "With braziers to set us alight. Sir Jean of Chartres and his squire are setting up a line of pikemen along our rail, with crossbowmen in the castles fore and aft."

He said this with an air of quiet assessment, always a man to comment on the balance of a lance, or the enemy's formation, as though he himself could not bleed. But while Sir Nigel impressed me with his cheer, even now sniffing the sea breeze with a show of spirit, Rannulf's calculating coolness stirred no love in me. During the massacre of two thousand prisoners Rannulf had joined in, showing our footmen how to cut out the guts of unarmed folk.

"The brave Jean of Chartres, able to fight at last," said Nigel. "We should have sorted sergeants from squires before this."

We should have decided which knight would command in a battle, he meant, and which fighters would be subordinate. Sir Nigel and Sir Rannulf had ordered much of the camp, and even footmen who could not understand a word of English would jump to Sir Nigel's commands.

Now an arrow lifted from the enemy galley, high into the fading blue sky.

And splintered on the deck.

THREE

Arrows hummed.

Such missiles in flight can be things of beauty. But a recent and just-forgotten hatred of such objects stirred in me, awakened from the long hours of siege, the heat and suffocating dust of the battle. I was not alone in this feeling. Arrows clattered on the deck, and angry feet kicked at them, sending them spinning along the planks.

Osbert scrambled for one, and seized it—a pale, goose-feathered arrow with a black iron tip—a Norman arrow, now returned to us by the Infidel archers.

Sir Nigel would have clapped a reassuring hand on my shoulder, but in his injured state he rested his hand gently on my arm. "No knight loves a sea fight, but we'll sweat them, Hubert."

As the two enemy galleys drew close, the hiss of the racing water was nearly louder than my own thoughts. I believed that all of us would join Nigel in Heaven, and I wished my parents could see me as I was then, hale and unhurt, before the fighting cut me down.

Our galley was longer, with stouter timbers than her opponents'.

This meant that she was strong, but heavy, and our rowers could not keep this pace. With a shouted command, the oars on one side of the vessel were shipped, dripping and gleaming, and withdrawn in a breathtaking show of sea training, each oar run in while the oars on the opposite side lashed the water.

We braced for what was coming.

The collision knocked most of us off our feet.

Edmund gave me a hand, pulling me upright from the deck. Our crossbowmen climbed to any perch they could reach and sent a rain of missiles down into the *gallea*. I had no sight of attacking boarders, only the working shoulders and heads of our own pikemen and knights as they stabbed forward with their weapons, their cries a low rumble, curses and battle exhortations in a dozen languages.

Osbert climbed to a high point on the galley castle and balanced himself as he drew a bow and sent the Norman arrow down into the attackers. Other archers joined him, and ship's boys shot unidentifiable objects, pork bones, and leaden sling-slugs down into the enemy. Sleek as they were, the Saracen ships were lower in the water, and our men could strike downward, into the faces of the attackers.

Rannulf tapped my shoulder, and in the heavy surge of

cries and involuntary groans I could not hear what he was saying. I followed his glance. The vessel on our seaward side had shot ahead and was backing oars, laboring furiously to close on us.

Crusaders not yet engaged in fighting now made a great display of courage for the benefit of this new attacker, slashing at the air with swords, gesturing with axes and battle hammers. I knew how much of this was, for many, empty show, injured and disease-wasted men acting as though what they wanted most was to wet their swords in enemy blood. We yelled and shook our weapons, voices muffled by helmets.

The approaching *gallea* seemed to be a many-legged creature unable to decide its course of attack. Too close to gain momentum to spike us with her rams, too far off to grapple with us and trade blows, the attacker's oars clashed with ours. Enemy oars snapped, splinters spinning high into the air. Most of our own, much stouter oars remained straight out from the ship, keeping the enemy from closing on us.

I stayed beside Sir Nigel, to keep him from taking the brunt of any outthrust weapon, and to his right was Rannulf, ready, likewise, to fend off blows. Sir Nigel climbed onto the rail, and as I clung to the skirt of the chain mail to keep him steady, fear made my breath come in tight-throated gasps. I know of no one who can swim—the art is not taught in England—and I dreaded lest I or one of my companions tumble over the side.

His example encouraged the others. Edmund brandished his war hammer in the faces of the enemy, bearded men, their heads swathed in white fabric. A few of the Saracen halberds reached across the gap, long weapons, half ax and half pike, made for smashing helmeted heads. Even at this awkward distance the weapons found targets, and my feet slipped twice, until at last I went down hard. In the dimming light I caught the gleam of shiny darkness spreading underfoot as I lay on the deck.

Glowing coals snapped through the air, delivered by a catapult somewhere on the enemy deck, and the ship's mates were busy, dumping buckets of water over the sizzling embers and spreading sand to soak up the blood.

I felt a strong grip on my arm, and Edmund helped me to my feet.

"Are you hurt?" he asked anxiously.

I murmured that I had slipped, nothing more than that.

"Thank God!" said Edmund fervently, and, as so often before, I was grateful to have such a friend.

The darkness became more perfect, the last dull glow of vanishing sun reflected on our weapons, and even as knights and squires began to crumple, unable to stand against the assault, some rhythm changed in the urgency of the fighting, Crusaders no longer calling out for Our Lord's help.

The galley's timbers groaned as we freed ourselves from one attacking vessel. Pikemen shoved off the other craft. The enemy's taunts continued to sound menacing, but a new tone had entered the engagement. Our vessel was moving. Edmund had to take care to keep his balance, putting one hand out to the rail, and two armored bodies crashed to the deck with the distinctive chiming thud of chain-mailed men.

The sea was gliding under us as we left our attackers behind.

The *Sint Markt* was aflame far off.

The burning ship reflected in the black water, and even as our captain ordered sails set, I heard Edmund say that we could not leave so many behind.

"We leave them to Heaven's embrace," said Sir Nigel, his voice a rasp.

We were not free yet. While our former pursuers fell away, new ones arrived, judging by the sound and the white flash of sea around distant oars, the pace of the rowers steady.

Sailors mopped up the red plaster at our feet, a paste of blood and sand.

Enemy galleys were keeping our pace, and I kept the sword in my hand.

FOUR

We stayed ready all night.

By dawn the wind behind us was stiff, and two enemy galleys followed us against the rising sun. Our oars remained inactive, the weather-bleached lateen sail driving the ship, buckets of bread and wine lowered down through the hatches to the rowers. They lounged about below, laughing and talking like any group of laborers.

The seamen adjusted sail, coiled rope, all with a show of carelessness, but every one of us observed the enemy craft, indistinct shapes on the gray sea. A few men had died of wounds during the night, and a priest's clerk, the holiest person on the ship, spoke the appropriate Latin as the linen-draped bodies were eased into the water. The clerk himself coughed between prayers and had to support himself against the freeboard long after the dead had vanished beneath the white-capped swells.

Edmund had suffered seasickness on his earliest voyage, but he seemed immune to the ailment now. A few men coughed up the ship's bread and pale wine they had taken in, but most were sound enough, perhaps because menace concentrated their thoughts. One enemy vessel dropped away, into the silver horizon, but the other crept closer.

"A ship is no place for my sort of fight," said Rannulf, taking a swallow of his morning wine. "There's no place for the lance—"

"And certainly no place for a horse," said Sir Nigel.

Sir Nigel said this without a trace of amusement, but I could not keep the picture from my mind—a knight trying to aim a lance onboard a tossing galley while his nervous mount spilled him. I stifled my laugh, making a single inward cluck, sounding, I am afraid, like a brood hen, and Edmund's cheeks reddened slightly. We avoided looking at each other. I was sure that, spurred by our relief at being alive, we would burst into unseemly laughter.

Sir Nigel gave us a friendly frown. "What do you two know of lance work?" he chided gently.

"My lord, too little, indeed," said Edmund earnestly. *Too lytle, sertayn.*

Edmund was coarser born than I, the son of a staver, a man who cut slats and sold them to coopers to be made into barrels. Edmund had been apprenticed to the once much-respected Otto, royal moneyer, who had been arrested and killed for coining debased silver. Edmund himself had barely escaped brutal punishment. Throughout our journeys together, an inner seriousness kept Edmund eager to learn, as though he might fail in his duties as squire and find himself in prison again. It was not impossible. If Edmund returned to England with reports that he had not fought with honor, the king's men could order him into chains.

Edmund lacked a family name. I, on the other hand, was known as Hubert of Bakewell, and sometimes Hubert Simonson, although I would have loved to have a more legendary-sounding name. Knights and even squires were honored by surnames endowed by their masters or fellow knights, like the well-known warriors William Sans Peur—"without fear"—Alan Dur de Main, and Harold Longsword. Men did not give themselves such names, except, perhaps, within their own hearts. Otherwise an army would be filled with names like Tom Striketerror or Hubert Fearnaught.

"You think yourselves the stuff of knights," said Sir Nigel, laughing gently, "but you two both are upstart fledglings."

"Give us lances, my lord," I said, speaking for the two of us, "and let us meet any enemy."

Sir Nigel gave me a good-natured smile, but there was a sadness about him. We had all left friends behind in the Holy Land, and perhaps Nigel felt a lingering sorrow that battle had not claimed his soul during the night.

But this was the first time that Sir Nigel had put into words the hope Edmund and I shared—that we were, in truth, the stuff of knighthood. Surely fledglings grow into full-feathered cocks. It was true that Edmund knew too little about weapons. Knights practice lance work by tilting at the quintain—charging into a span of wood from which hung, on one end, a shield, and on the other a weighted sack. I had practiced the skill myself in England, and during my many months of training as a squire. Edmund had been named a squire just before we all left on the Crusade, and such training, and much else, would be required for Edmund to ripen into knighthood.

"If Heaven wills it," Sir Nigel was saying, "Rannulf will teach Edmund how to carry a lance, and train Hubert in how to hold his tongue."

"With pleasure," said Rannulf, without the trace of a smile. Edmund had attended this famous knight, while I counted myself fortunate to have served Nigel.

I liked to imitate Rannulf behind his back sometimes, forcing Edmund to laugh at his master despite himself. Rannulf's stony expressions were legendary, and I doubted he took pleasure in food or drink, or passing water, or even attending to an itch.

While most fighting men are close-cropped and clean shaven, Rannulf was bearded, his mouth sword-scarred. He was called Rannulf of Josselin, after the famous joust in that city where he killed six men. Both Rannulf and Nigel were bachelor knights who owned no or little land, and lived well and honorably by hiring themselves to noblemen.

Sir Nigel's reputation convinced my father to pay him to school me in the ways of knighthood. My father would never have struck such an arrangement with Sir Rannulf. Now that Edmund had battle trove in the chest, along with the rest of us, it was truly possible that both of us had gold enough to complete the training someday, and purchase the war-kit needed to become men-at-arms.

But then my thoughts were interrupted by Sir Jean and Nicholas, dragging a third man between them.

"Your manservant," said Nicholas, looking Edmund in the eye, "is a thief."

Nicholas held Osbert by the arm. Edmund's servant tried to look as dignified as he could, forced as he was into a crab-like stoop.

"Nay, my lord Edmund," protested Osbert, "I am no such creature."

"His hand was in my gipser," said Nicholas, indicating the leather purse on his belt. Such gipser purses are usually carried by franklins and town worthies with enough coin to make them necessary—most squires would find a belt purse inconvenient in the rough-and-tumble of a voyage.

Squires and shield bearers glanced our way, and a few gathered, but most of the ship's passengers drowsed, drank wine, or sweated off fever.

"Osbert is a worthy servant," said Edmund formally, "and no thief, on my honor."

"On your honor," echoed Nicholas.

Edmund had spoken well, but hastily. Osbert had joined Edmund since the battle, and none of us knew his past.

But the assertion having been made, I stepped to Osbert and took his other arm. "And on mine," I added, trying to keep my voice steady.

This was all *hyg speche,* high speech, artificial and courtly. It was also, I thought, a little foolish. Osbert had quick hands, and an eager-to-please manner I did not trust.

Sir Nigel and Sir Rannulf looked on, their mouths set. Knights did not involve themselves in disagreements among squires, unless to protect a valued squire's life, but neither did our two masters absent themselves, as many would have done. They remained, aloof but very much a presence, witnessing what was said.

"I saw the thief at work," said Sir Jean.

Sir Jean's surcoat had been stained with old blood along the hem, but now it was spattered with drying gore—and worse.

"Anyone, my lord, would run from a sight such as yourself," I offered, hoping I struck the proper joking tone.

Sir Jean had a heavy glance. My teachers had explained to me that vision originates in our eyes, sight emitting from our eyeballs the way rays of light beam outward from a lantern. I had asked Father Giles what happened when we closed our eyes—did the sunny world go dark?

But under the gaze of Sir Jean it was easy to believe, once again, that Father Giles was right. The eye is a source of power—in this case, withering my will. I summoned a glance of my own, and breathed an inward prayer for Heaven's strength.

"What was taken by this thief, good Sir Jean?" asked Sir Nigel.

I wanted to protest.

But Sir Nigel gave me a small signal I had learned to watch for—a tiny dip of his chin, a slight shift of his eye, all directed at me. Sometimes I speak when I should not, unable to rein in my breath. But now I proved my worth by keeping silent.

"It was the attempt that gives offense," said Sir Jean.

"Leave the servant to us," said Sir Rannulf carefully through his sword-scarred lips. It was easy to see why man and knight both respected such a voice, as though a gnarled, storm-lashed tree had been given the power of speech.

The serving man rolled his eyes and grimaced in purest terror.

"We'll work a confession out of him," said Rannulf, "if he hides any sin. And feed him justice."

"You'll see that he confesses?" asked Sir Jean.

"With cord and sticks," said Sir Rannulf.

This referred to a simple device, and an effective torture, one I had seen at work in Nottingham, where the town executioner is an adept at separating men from their secrets. Two sticks are connected by a leather thong. The cord circles the offender's head, and the twin sticks are twisted tight until, if no confession starts, the leather cinch compresses the bones of the head.

Edmund and I were livid, quivering with silent protest, kept from blurting a word by a cool look from Sir Nigel.

Osbert sobbed.

Squire Nicholas leaned toward Sir Jean, murmuring into his ear.

Sir Jean looked Edmund up and down, like a man doubtful of the value of a dray mare. "I hear this squire was a counterfeiter's apprentice."

Sir Rannulf tossed the last of his wine overboard, and let the cup fall to the deck.

He put his hand on his sword.

FIVE

"Edmund Strongarm served God with King Richard's army," said Rannulf, speaking slowly and emphatically.

Edmund Strongarm.

I thrilled at the sound of this—the first time anyone had called my friend such a glorious name. Edmund himself showed no outward emotion, but prickles of pink appeared on his cheek.

"And like any Crusading sinner," said Sir Nigel, "his past crimes, whatever they might have been, are washed clean."

Sir Jean stood as tall as he could—he was a big man—and I had a flash of sympathy for him. Like many knights, he was grieved to be leaving the war, and he wanted any possible way to assert his pride.

Nicholas released Osbert. The manservant sprawled on the deck, and then he attempted to be equal to the dignity of a squire-at-arms's service. He stood upright, pulling at his tunic.

Sir Jean put his hands on his hips. "Let me hear the servant confess," he said.

"We'll attend to this," said Sir Nigel, "in our own time." And then Nigel laughed and made an openhanded gesture. "Share some wine with me, each of you."

The weather was sharpening, waves higher, the wind behind us strong and cold, our sail straining at its ropes.

Edmund and I had arranged a place against the rail, a canopy of canvas, a worn sailcloth on the deck. Sir Nigel offered the serving man a cup of wine, and Osbert drank gratefully. Sir Nigel found a knob of bread wrapped in a blanket—hard, dry ship's fare—and broke off a piece for all of us before he ate any himself.

"The next time, Edmund, such an accusation is voiced, your man will bleed," said Nigel. The loss of a hand, or an entire limb, was common punishment for stealing, often followed by public hanging. "Guilty or innocent, it will not matter."

"You will not force a confession?" asked Edmund.

It was a surprise to me to hear Rannulf chuckle, a low, almost silent laugh.

Sir Nigel would have laughed, too, I believe, but did not want to offend his two earnest squires. "Surely, Hubert, you and Edmund don't think that I pay any heed to a Chartrian too stubborn to put on clean clothes?"

———

"Of course you're equal to the name," I insisted.

I wondered if Heaven would forgive me for the sin of envy. It was true that I had been a loyal squire to Nigel long before Edmund had stepped across our threshold, and I knew that I was much quicker with a sword. And yet Edmund was the sort of fighting man people follow with their eyes. I believed that while in future battles I would be brave enough, and quick to parry, slice, and cut, piles of dead enemies would heap up around Edmund.

We stood high in the stern castle, gazing into the stiff salt wind. One enemy ship followed us, a loyal shadow.

"Someday," he said, "I'll become equal to the name, with God's grace."

I swelled myself up, swelling out my chest. *"Let mee heer heem con-fess,"* I said, sounding, I must confess, every bit exactly like Sir Jean.

"There were flies on his blouse," said Edmund, as though confiding a secret. Knights were generally discussed with respect, even in private.

I laughed.

I had Edmund laughing with my further imitation of Sir Jean, big with pride as I gazed about.

And then the dogged enemy craft drew my full attention. "Do you think she will catch us?" I asked.

Edmund considered. He looked up at the blue sky, judging the weather.

I wanted her to run us down, just then. I wanted another

enemy to attack us so that I, too, might win a name. *Hubert Quicksword*. "Why do they keep rowing and rowing after us—why not turn back?"

"Faith," he said.

He even spoke more like a knight than I did. He was often solemn and used few words, while I chattered, tried to make people laugh, and was in every way a more feather-weight squire.

"I'll wager," I said, "the silver thimble I found that we'll be fighting again by sunset."

Gambling had been forbidden in the Crusader camp, and now that we were aboard ship the deck was alive with the rattle of dice. I had discovered the silver thimble on the battlefield, long after the fighting was over, among the wreckage of horseflesh and weaponry. Both Saracens and Crusaders used thimbles and thread to repair everything from clothing to saddle work, but a silver thimble decorated with stars and crescent moons was a treasure.

"I'll not accept your wager, Hubert."

"My thimble against the silver cup Osbert found under the dead—" To speak of dead horses was to remind Edmund of the noble Winter Star, a mount I knew he still mourned.

"The cup is made of trade silver," he protested, "half brass. Three bent old cups like that would equal one of your thimbles." A moneyer's apprentice knows alloy from ore, and amber from glass.

Edmund was honest, too, the way knights were expected to be and rarely were. No wonder Rannulf admired him, and Nigel, too. "Take the bet, Edmund," I said, with too much feeling.

"If it pleases you," he said hesitantly.

" 'If it pleases me!' " I said, exasperated, imitating him quite well—capturing his note of manly caution, that solid, clear-minded common sense that I had come to love and depend on, but which at the moment I could not tolerate.

"Do you think Osbert is a thief?" asked Edmund in a soft voice.

"Of course he is," I responded, with little regard for what I said. "There can be no doubt. You saw him snatch that arrow off the deck yesterday. No one has such quick hands but a sworn pickpocket."

Edmund blinked. "I trust him, Hubert."

What could I respond? I was ashamed of my own tongue, and wiped my hand across my lips.

SIX

Later that day the wind out of the east was cold, and Edmund and I huddled in our wool cowls.

Not so many days ago I had sat sweating in a Crusader tent, in heat I was sure would never end. In the long hours of the siege I had used the handle of a knife to crush lice hiding in the seam of my tunic, and when I had asked Edmund if he could recall ever being cold—truly cold—he had chuckled and agreed that it seemed impossible such a thing could be.

And now here it was, a true chill, and I did indeed find it refreshing.

The stiff breeze allowed the ship to cut through waves, and often during the day rowers from below climbed up through the hatch and walked among us, muscular men looking both well fed and at ease. I remarked to Sir Nigel that the oarsmen looked happy, considering that they were imprisoned felons, and Sir Nigel responded that a wise captain would feed and water every rower with care. He added that some leaders shared prize money from captured enemy vessels with the rowers, along with the rest of the crew.

"If the Infidel should catch us at sea," said Nigel, "we'll think ourselves lucky if they chain us to an oar."

For the first time since we left the Holy Land, there was the bright sound of several men joining in laughter. A very large rat had startled a cook's mate, the beast darting out of a sack of flour. The creature proceeded to cause startled cries and relieved laughter wherever it scampered.

"I thought it was a devil!" cried a shield bearer sheepishly.

And no Saracen ship was likely to capture any of us. Edmund had been right—there was no further sea battle. The enemy vessel broke off its pursuit by midafternoon, as we looked on. The long, low warship turned in a single, swift move—no vessel can turn about as quickly as a galley—and in a few heartbeats she had set a course for the north.

"She'll harass the shipping out of Constantinople," said Sir Nigel when we reported this development to him. "And I pray God's mercy on anyone they meet."

For the first time I felt reassured that Sir Nigel was relieved to be alive, and beginning to relish the thought of sizzling mutton and a warm bed.

Edmund shook his head and laughed, but I insisted—I owed him silver.

Osbert was seated on our trove chest, a short sword at his hip, and he leaped aside when I said I needed to withdraw a bit of our riches.

"I have lost a wager," I added without a trace of sorrow.

"But you'll win your share again another day, my lord," said Osbert, eager as ever to please.

I struggled with the large lock, tarnished and heavy. When I had the chest open at last, I rummaged inside, searching among the silk-wrapped treasures. Searched, and paused. And rummaged more quickly.

"Osbert, where is the rest of our booty?" I asked.

"My lord, it is all in the chest, I pray, where it belongs."

Osbert's manner was enough to move a footstool to fury. It was never proper to address a squire as *my lord,* and I found this simply another example of Osbert's oily behavior. Nevertheless, for the sake of Edmund, I treated Osbert with steady good manners when I said, "Has Sir Rannulf removed anything from the chest?"

Osbert put both hands to his breast. "I can say that he has not, good Hubert," he answered in a trembling voice.

Edmund joined me in gazing into the open trunk. He searched slowly, and then more urgently, through a chest that should have been full of wrapped and padded prizes, but was now nearly half empty.

"Hubert, it's true," Edmund exclaimed at last. "Someone has stolen our treasure!"

seven

Osbert was on his knees before us, his hands held pleadingly in the half-dark of the ship's hold.

"I know nothing of any missing riches," he said. He added, "I swear it on every holy thing."

Efrec halydam. Even a thoroughly bedeviled thief would be reluctant to swear such an oath, unless he spoke the truth.

"I loyally serve my lord Edmund and all his fellows," Osbert was saying, "and would do no hurt to any of you." He turned his head slightly, and looked up at me from an angle. "Besides, you don't see a new-hatched fool before you, good Hubert. Why would I steal treasure from the very men most able to skin me alive?"

"Some creatures take such risks," I said. Edmund stayed close to me, perhaps ready to stay my hand if I could not keep my temper.

"I'm a sinner, like most other men," said Osbert. "I'll play ram to any lady's ewe, by my faith. But I am no thief."

"If you say it often enough, you'll convince yourself," I retorted, but my ill humor was softening. Osbert had a way of gazing hopefully, like a pup with his head to one side. If it was nothing more than a false display of innocence, it was certainly ingenious. Osbert was the one ready with a pitcher of sweet wine, or reaching to pluck a weevil from the crust of bread one was about to devour.

The servant had the gift of being easy to like. It was a powerful charm. I helped Osbert to his feet, and he said, "Thank you, my—" He was about to say *my lord*. "Hubert, I thank you."

"Someone stole your thimble, nonetheless," said Edmund.

"And your cup," I said.

Rannulf and Nigel looked on, as grim-faced as any two knights in Christendom. Sir Rannulf's possessions were intact, his collection of scimitars at the bottom of the chest untouched, and Sir Nigel's sacks of coins were likewise nestled toward the corners of the trunk, and largely safe. Edmund and I had suffered the keenest losses, although whoever had stolen the goods had been hasty—much of our silver remained, and the two of us were still much wealthier than when we had set forth from Nottingham months before.

"Some thief did his work during the fighting," said Edmund. "That was the only sure opportunity."

"Not every servant is an honest one, my lords," said Osbert.

Nigel put a hand on my shoulder, his grip steadier than it

had been the day before. During the recent sea battle he had done little more than look on, his sword lashed to his grip, as he called effective directives to the fighters. "Some sinner will pay a price for this, Hubert."

One's soul is a pearl of great price, and Christ's death was the price of our redemption. *Price* was the secret of each dawning, and each sunset, all of it bought with Our Lord's blood. I knew that Sir Nigel meant something extraordinary with this remark, but I did not guess that even now he was prepared to sacrifice his life.

In the several remaining days of our voyage to Chios, the passengers were quiet, but it was a simmering silence. Even the dullest member of the ship's crew must have been aware that Sir Nigel kept staring icily across the ship at Sir Jean, and that the big Chartrian knight made no attempt to look away or hide his disdain. It was plain to all of us that Sir Nigel believed, on no particular evidence, that Sir Jean and his manservants were guilty of the crime.

It did seem that Sir Jean had more weight in his belt purse now, and that Nicholas gave his own gipser a pat from time to time. Surely Sir Jean's gaze was showing off some secret triumph over us. He smiled and made remarks that had his servants laughing, and made a show of trying to kick Osbert with his good leg whenever Edmund's servant scurried past.

"The knight needs a lesson in virtue," Nigel remarked one evening, "taught from the back of a horse."

The few gnarled chickens brought along for food were served up in a thin, stringy stew. The bread, which had always been scant and stony, ran out long before the wine. There was plenty of that, both sweet and tart, so for the last day of our journey squires staggered about, stumbling and vomiting, but without much talk or laughter, all of us chilled by the growing enmity between Sir Nigel and Sir Jean.

A few more Crusaders died of fever or wounds, and the priest's clerk succumbed, too, and was buried at sea with brief prayers spoken by a knight from Bremen as the wind drove us. The white-bearded captain directed us to be cheer-ful—the ship was good, the port was near, or some such—I could never make out a single word, and I have some abil-ity with unfamiliar tongues.

My father had sailed as a young man, delivering lana-cloth—woven wool—to the merchants of the Low Coun-tries and the Seine. Just as he had taught me to take an interest in cloth and drapery, he had taught me to love ships, from the spruce mast to the rummage of the hold. But every time the oars ran out to assist the power of the sail, I was all the more convinced that I would rather travel by sail alone than by the strength of a rower's back.

Islands rose and sank behind us. The smell of land was often in the air, but a foreign, sun-stunned scent, herbs and dry plow land.

On the Feast of Saint Denis—the saint usually pictured carrying his own serenely smiling severed head—we ap-proached our harbor. We had seen other mountaintops pass us by and had gazed across the windy sea at the dim impression of other harbors, fishing boats skimming the water.

Now, after less than a week, the oars swept us steadily toward a tawny, rocky range of brown land. The faraway sounds of voices and song reached us.

Edmund and I leaned excitedly over the rail, watching the land approach. It unfolded from a flat, promising range of hills, to a place with depth, valleys and woods. A child ran along the shore with a dog—or a small horse. Or some other creature I knew nothing about. The world was filled with wondrous creatures, like the heathens Father Giles once described to me, with eyes in the palms of their hands.

"Father Giles explained to me about the fall of Troy," I said, hastily trying to recall what Greek I might have learned. While I had scratched out my Roman *puella* and *puer* on a *tabela*, a student hornbook, I had seen the Greek alphabet only on a single vellum scroll. Father Giles, who had studied with scholars in Ireland, had declared that the Greeks had invented fighting as knights knew it, lining up in a long row of lances and charging into an opposing, equally eager enemy. "He told me a Greek warrior-chief would not take a single step on a journey without consulting the Delphic oracle."

"I thought you could recite Greek backward."

"I can, indeed," I said.

Edmund made a show of waiting expectantly, and we both laughed.

Rocky hills rose skyward, groves of gray-green trees in the distance. A goat somewhere bleated, and a cow or sheep bell clattered. A village of white houses embraced a sunny harbor, crowded with the bare masts and webbed rigging of sailing ships. While Venice and Constantinople were the major ports of the Crusade, Chios was another traditional harbor, thriving now with everything from ship repairs to provender for the distant war, crates of honeycomb and leathery stacks of salt fish.

Blue-black mounds of charcoal were shoveled into sacks, and spools of hempen cordage were wheeled along the quay. On an overlook, wooden scaffolding and a half-built stone wall showed where a castle was being erected, tower masons pausing to shield their eyes and watch the *San Raffaello* as she kissed the wharf.

But before a single man could disembark, Sir Nigel marched across the deck and delivered an insult to Sir Jean.

"Let us see," said my master, "if a Frankish knight can fight as well as he can steal."

EIGHT

It was what I had been waiting for—hard words, one knight to the other—but it was a shock to hear them.

Sir Jean stiffened, and for an instant his big, petulant features looked sincerely puzzled, an expression that made him seem momentarily appealing, like a boy unable to comprehend adult speech. Nicholas, beside him, made a show of stepping before his master protectively. Sir Nigel turned on his heel and marched back through the startled throng, a pleased expression on his face.

The land beneath our feet was so steady it mocked our sea-addled strides—Edmund and I had to put a hand out to each other as we stumbled. Women stepped aside as we stiff-legged our way to a well, then let the bucket fall into the shaft with an echoing splash. Everyone knows that water is a source of serious illness, but after days of salt air Edmund and I both drank deeply, letting the water spill.

The village was sun-soaked, the air sweet. Donkeys, animals like stout little horses, observed us with gentle gazes. Women opened shutters, and partly closed them as we passed. Young women saw us and lowered their eyes. They wore bright red or yellow girdles about their waists, and flowing white garments. Older women, handsome and mysterious, spied at us from beneath bright-woven shawls. I felt my heart quicken at every street crossing, at every wellhead, with the notes of far-off female song.

Sir Nigel strode ahead of us, as he liked to do, and secured lodging for us in an inn beside a huge, spreading tree. The proprietors were a man and wife, who peered at us with a kind of cautious pity that made me both proud to be a Crusader, and annoyed. Why should they pity us?

"Not everyone envies men-at-arms," said Edmund as we explored a neighboring field later that day. "Perhaps many folk would rather sleep under a peaked roof than travel with a sword."

The farmland here was thick with dust, walls of mossless stone thrown up where I expected to see hedgerows and cow-mucky ponds. Bees tasted thistle flowers, and vineyards were festooned with tar-dark bunches of grapes.

Large columns of stone lay among the weeds. Father Giles had told me about the Greek knight Achilles, and the travels of the knight-errant Ulysses, and had explained that the ancients worshiped gods and goddesses in temples of marble. A goat perched on the stump of a column and made no sound as we approached.

"Was there a famous siege here?" asked Edmund, refer-
ring to the ruined columns, half hidden by grasses.

"No doubt," I ventured.

Edmund drank in the sight of the marble ruins and nodded. "In the time of our great-grandfathers."

"Longer ago, I think."

He wondered at this.

The earthy clods made a comforting sound under our
feet, and birds chattered and bickered in the twisting arms of
a fig tree. The happy song of these starlings, much like the
familiar birds of home, emboldened me to mention the subject uppermost in my mind.

"Maybe no harm will come of Nigel's insult," I said.

Sometimes Edmund takes a long moment before he
responds, as though thoughts were leaden pigs—ingots of
raw metal, difficult to move. One of the virtues I love best
in Edmund is his deep study of any question I put to him.

"It's possible," he said skeptically, "that Sir Jean will ignore
Nigel's offense—but not likely. Knights love a fight."

"Better than wine," I agreed.

"I think neither of us will ever be perfect cowards," he
added. "But I think Nigel and Rannulf both love bloody
steel more than we do."

Edmund had tolerated the human wreckage of massacre
and battle better than I, and with his height and broad
shoulders he was perhaps better suited to war. But I was by
far the better hand with sword and buckler, and could sit a
horse more easily.

"If you had to lead a band of young squires into battle," I
said, "what would you tell them?"

"Squires as pitifully ignorant as I used to be?"

"As bare of experience," I responded with a laugh, "as both of us were."

"I wouldn't tell them anything," he said, watching the starlings take flight from the fig tree. "Every word ever told about war is a lie."

He turned to me and smiled. "There were five birds just then. A blessed omen, no doubt."

It's true that five is one of the sacred numbers. Christ suffered five wounds on Good Friday, and people hoping for lucky omens count birds, moths around a candle, and even flea bites, hoping the fortunate number will show itself.

That's another thing I like and admire about my friend—he is more devout than I am and, without knowing it, shows me the way to Heaven's favor.

When we returned to the inn, spearmen were stationed at street corners, sent forth by the local nobles to protect the town from Crusading warriors. They were a thin, mousy bunch of guards, older men with tight, unhappy faces, and young men who would not meet our eyes. It never failed to impress and amuse me how ordinary villagers feared Crusaders, even a pair of novice men-at-arms like ourselves.

That evening, after a dish of roast lamb and fat capons, and enough red wine to heal the soul, Nicholas came before us, dressed in his finest kirtle and belt, his sword at his hip. He stood erect, one hand on his sword hilt, exactly the way a squire is trained to appear when delivering important tidings.

"My lord," he sang out, "the worshipful and God-fearing Christian knight Sir Jean of Chartres requests an apology from Sir Nigel."

Nigel said nothing.

Nicholas waited several heartbeats. Then he continued, "My lord challenges Sir Nigel to an ordeal of arms."

It was my duty to respond to these words on behalf of my master, but I could not remember the appropriate formula. Such challenges were the stuff of poetry. No one uttered them in real life—or so I tried to believe.

Besides, it was hard to take the message seriously in my wine-cozened condition. The air was sweet with the smell of hill spices, thyme and sweet basil and other herbs considered precious in an English garden, and here as common as weeds. The growing dark was cool, but the spreading tree and the music of the village around us so welcoming that none of us wanted to retire to our cots. A single lamp of clay burned with a gentle feather of smoke, the olive-oil flame giving off a warm perfume.

I nearly offered Nicholas a place at our table. Edmund gazed with one hand on the wine pitcher, Rannulf leaning forward to hear what I would say. I was taking too long to shape a response.

Nicholas waited, giving me his smile, chin forward, the one that meant he was superior to me in every way. And yet it was not a purely arrogant smile. It let me see that at some other time, on another island, he and I could have been friends. I half believed that Nicholas was tempted to unfasten his sword belt and join us in the lamplight.

But Sir Nigel set down his wine cup and stood.

I recalled my duty, and rose with him.

"On behalf of my most worshipful Christian lord and master," I began. I couldn't remember the rest.

Nigel glanced at me. *Go on.*

I summoned the words, battling the effects of the wine. I continued on, reciting the phrases, more or less, that were customary in accepting a challenge. I left out the phrase *God-fearing,* perhaps not willing to use the word *fear.* Otherwise I had the phrasing in something like the proper order, and I pronounced the Frankish words as well as possible.

All the while, through the fumes of the wine, I began to realize that the words were not mere language.

I accepted the challenge that could cause Nigel's death.

nine

A joust would take a few days to arrange properly, but everyone was eager to see the thing done right, just as it would have been done in Flanders or Saxony. There was no reluctance to do battle—there was a desire, as Rannulf put it, "to see that the greatest amount of harm might be done when the fighting starts."

We had no chargers—no warhorses of any kind. An elderly knight from Poitou, overseeing the construction of the castle, provided capable mounts, for a price. Nigel had sold his battle lance in the Holy Land to a Cretan knight whose weapons had been stolen by skirmishing Bedouins. New lances, too, were provided by the Poitevin knight for the appropriate amount of silver. Sir Nigel insisted that he would need time to examine various sites for the forthcoming contest, and Sir Jean quickly consented to any necessary delay.

I set to work, shaking out the inevitable kinks in Sir Nigel's chain mail, inspecting the bridle and saddle as I had been trained to do. Sir Nigel's horse, a rough-haired stallion the Greek handlers called Nereus, shied at my touch, flared his nostrils, and made one of those magnificent horse sneezes that blast the air out of the stables. I called on Edmund to help, and he soothed the animal with a single whisper.

"Sir Nigel's bones have not healed," I said, speaking in a quiet voice as I readied the leather trappings, the handle of the shield, the inner lining of the helmet. Even the lowliest plowman could estimate the amount of time it took for Heaven to accomplish its will: three months, three weeks, three days for a sow to farrow; three fortnights for a broken bone to mend.

"He's been tossing stones against a wall," said Edmund pensively. "Big cobbles from the beach."

It had been less than a month since Sir Nigel's injury. I could not speak for a moment, I was so filled with feeling.

"Nigel will depend on you," said Edmund.

"No doubt," I offered, "Sir Jean is not as murderous as they say."

"I hear he's a cruel man," said Edmund unhappily, "and a sure-handed killer."

I ran a comb over my own warhorse, a gray and brown spotted creature named Proteus. My mount gave every indication of great calm, and I was sure no amount of effort would ever get it to act like a proper charger. Squires were expected to fight in light armor, squire against squire, on less impressive mounts.

I knew full well that I would be required to attend my master in the joust—perhaps go so far as to do some fighting myself. Even though I had studied sword work with the best tutors my father could afford, the thought made the spleen run thin in my body.

"I believe Nicholas is one of those proud squires," I said hopefully, "who can't handle a sword."

"I would fear him as much as Sir Jean," said Edmund with a dogged earnestness.

I flung away the comb and seized Edmund by the shoulders. "You are choosing your words very unwisely, Edmund," I said. "With a great lack of tact," I added, wishing I could laugh—or weep.

"I am praying for you, Hubert," said Edmund, surprised by my sudden outburst.

"Praying!" I was about to say that sacred words would not sharpen a lance or keep an untried horse from panic.

"To Saint Mark, who has blessed us all this long journey."

I had forgotten how uncommonly full of faith Edmund is, even in a world of devout and prayerful warriors. Surely his prayers go directly to the ears of the saints, while mine— if I may be forgiven for saying so—drift swallowlike, finding the way or not, as the wind wills.

I practiced with a dull sword, Edmund doing his best to imitate a knight's swordplay. The battle hammer is Edmund's best weapon—at sword work he could parry without ever gaining ground, strong enough, but with little cadence. I swung the blade until my arm was weak and the landscape swam in my vision. "More," Rannulf would say from one side, and finally take Edmund's place, driving me back, and back farther, showing me what real skill could do.

Osbert slipped into the stables, carrying a cloth heavy with cheese.

"Sir Jean is jousting at a fan, my lords," he confided. A fan was a form of quintain, easy to improvise, a shield on one end and a bag of sand on the other. "He got knocked off his horse once."

"Only once?" said Edmund unhappily.

"No more than that," said Osbert.

We shared the crumbly goat cheese, and washed it down with wine.

"He sent for a warhorse from Paris," Osbert added.

"It will take months," I protested, "for a horse to get here from—"

"He bought it from a Parisian ship bound for the Holy Land, and borrowed fine silver to pay for it. His servants saddled it this morning."

"And he fell off," I offered hopefully.

Osbert was a servant, but he was also an older man, and expected a trace of respect even from his masters. He gave me the sort of almost silent sigh teachers use when they are waiting for a young scholar's attention. "Wagering men wouldn't risk a bet on Sir Nigel, at first. He's admired and liked by every man who ever drew a blade, but he's too hurt, they say. I placed a few secret bets through my friends among the water bearers and the sergeants, if you'll forgive me, my lords."

Osbert paused meaningfully, cheese crumbs along his lower lip.

"What else, Osbert?" asked Edmund gently. He did not have a merchant's son's impatience with servants.

"I met an honest man from Beaune," he said. "A shield bearer, who lost a thumb outside of Acre."

Edmund ate cheese and sipped wine, listening with interest, but I was weary of waiting for Osbert to complete a thought. I said, "The thumb was stolen by Sir Jean, no doubt."

"Such an injury is a grievous one for a shield bearer, my lords," said Osbert.

"We'll pray for the soul of this thumb, Osbert," I said.

"And this shield man from Beaune," said Osbert, "is thought to be an expert at sword combat, my lords."

I didn't want to hear what Osbert was about to say.

Osbert had the grace to lower his voice. "I nearly struck the words out of his mouth with my fist, my lords. He says you'll make Nicholas de Foss sweat, my lord Hubert. But he'll stick your head on pike."

In the busy town where I spent my childhood, there were wealthy peasants, field folk who had worked the land for many generations and gradually prospered. Such men wore the finest homespun, not hairy cloth speckled with chaff but supple, pleated blouses, with ox-leather belts. Sometimes such monied farmers could afford a few ells of North Country wool, and they would enter my father's shop respectfully, pulling off their caps deferentially but paying king's coin, just like any franklin's wife. My mother made a point of remembering their children by name, although in truth most of them were either John or Lucy.

One such hardworking plower was Alf, a man I always associated with tireless labor and good cheer. He was always splitting a stump, or hanging a hog carcass from an oak. And one Michaelmas, Alf drank more ale than usual, and stumbled over a neighbor passed out drunk in the road.

The surgeon in Coneygate made Alf some wooden splints, and wrapped them so securely that he was able to steer a harrow and wave to any passerby even as his bones mended. I considered this, and reflected on Edmund's skill with his hands, whether mending a helmet or a delicate jewelry hasp.

I drew a sketch in the dirt. Wagons rumbled through the town, past the fountains, laden with jiggling mountains of black grapes, emerald grapes, pink grapes, the entire harvest of Chios beginning all at once.

I was concerned that Sir Nigel would shake his head and say that if Heaven willed him dead, then he would be dead. Nigel liked his wind rough and his wine tart, and tried to smile if something hurt him. Perhaps my master believed that a knight had to demonstrate unending *dureté*—toughness—to his squires. But to my great relief, he knelt and studied the sketch I had scratched in the sand.

"Brassards," I said, using the Frankish term for such armor. "Edmund can make one for each forearm."

"You think God will not strengthen me?" asked Nigel with a gentle laugh.

"God and your willing squire," I said.

Nigel smoothed his boot sole over the sketch.

"If it pleases you, Sir Nigel," I added urgently.

Nigel chuckled. "If it pleases *you*." But he gave a nod. "I will wear your *brassards* with gratitude." His bright eyes peered into mine. "And you, Hubert—is your sword arm ready?"

The morning of the joust was cold.

I had not slept, and neither had Edmund, we both admitted as we stepped out of the inn under the morning star. We each ate fresh brown bread in the early light, with honeycomb spread over the warm slices.

What words we utter, and what words we carefully do not say, can shift a day one way or another. Edmund made the sign of the cross, and his lips moved in silent prayer. I asked Heaven to heed what Edmund asked for, and to forgive my sins.

We went out to the place where, later that forenoon, the joust would take place. Frost-glazed thyme stroked our leggings. The flat, fallow field had been curried by the wind into an almost perfect surface, sun-baked but free of what folk in my town called *popples*—small stones. Knights preferred what Rannulf called a true fight, with no peaks or stumps to allow an advantage or hiding place.

I could not keep from feeling strangely detached, both myself and a stranger, like a court player paid to imitate me in a fete. My father employed such travelers on festival days, musicians and jongleurs from Derby. They wore pied-patterned leggings and colorful caps. I knew how the balladeer would describe me, his voice lifted handsomely in song:

Hubert, Squire Hubert, stands upon the field.
Where he will die.

TEN

I was afraid for myself, of course—many a squire has his liver lanced during a joust. But I was afraid, more than anything, for the life of my master.

Fear is a poison that makes the fingers cold, and the mouth dry. It is a great cause of sweat and of piss, and I found myself hurrying to the chamber pot all morning. It weakens the bowels, too, and it stirs the mind so badly that no single thought can settle. I was certain that the hour would never arrive, and in my anxiety half convinced myself that the long, slowly passing morning was proof that time was creaking, and falling still.

But the hour came.

Sir Nigel rode out into the sunlight.

He wore a brilliant blue cloak, bought especially for this

joust from a knight from Arles, and combed and mended by a fuller, one of many men who came forth to offer Sir Nigel their best help. It was held by an enameled clasp the shape of a lozenge. He wore a surcoat of finest white lamb's wool, a fabric that my father would have kept stored and brought out one bolt at a time for his most wealthy customers. I had fussed over the fabric and ordered the hem mended where a minuscule tear had marred one corner.

Sir Nigel carried his lance erect, the ashwood weapon sharpened with a soapstone and polished by my own hands, using the training drilled into me by stern and expert masters in the years when I could only dream of such tournaments. His shield was blue, decorated by the Crusader cross in white, polished by me to a satisfying luster. Wool clothing is rich with oil that accumulates on the hands, and I used it to bring out the light in the metals, and the glow in Nigel's leather. The shield hung from a jousting strap around his neck and over his left arm.

I carried Sir Nigel's helmet. The hair of his head had been close-cropped by a shearer from Whitby. Nigel's newly cut hair made him look younger, as did his bright gaze. Father Giles was right—the eye is the source of the world, and when someone like Sir Nigel closes his eyes, something is taken out of it.

Sir Jean's shield was scarlet, decorated with the symbol of a golden swift, a pair of stylized wings. Nicholas carried a standard, a muster flag of silk, that fluttered and tossed in the wind. The squire wore a surcoat of scarlet, and stabbed the standard into the earth, and plunged it in again, several times, until the rippling thing stayed where he wanted it, stuck into the field.

I carried no such standard, and the surcoat over my mail was the color of the sheep that had worn it on the hill, except for a fine blue border all around. Sir Nigel had said he preferred to spend his silver on wine and capons, and I tried to tell myself that I would turn the simplicity of my garment into a point of pride.

Sir Jean allowed his charger, a roan horse brushed until he gleamed, to high-step back and forth along the edge of the field. This process gave us long moments to admire the way Sir Jean sat in the saddle, and the firm way he carried his lance, but it was important that a horse be allowed to drop dung before heavy exertion. At last this necessity was accomplished, bright green-yellow manuring the dry land.

Sir Jean turned to one of his several sergeants and shield bearers, and motioned with a mailed hand. A crucifix on a long staff, the image of Our Lord, was carried out to him and held forth so that he might kiss it.

Knights and squires had attended Holy Mass at the edge of an olive grove, celebrated by an ailing English priest from the Genoan ship *Santa Croce*. The Greek priests practiced a dubious variety of Christ's creed, and Father Giles had warned me against worshiping in a sanctuary "not blessed by the Roman faith." When I had peered into a white-walled chapel, I had seen niches of flickering oil lamps, and a bronze-green visage of a saint or martyr imprisoned in a wooden frame. It was essential that men about to die draw their swords in a state of grace, and even now, as I cinched the saddle girth of Sir Nigel's horse just a little tighter, I was grateful that an Englishman—even one haggard from weeks of bowel flux—had blessed us.

I studied Sir Jean's ruddy face from a distance, looking for some trace of hesitation, some glimmer of doubt that honor required the death of at least one knight on this fine mid-morning, the sun warm, the air sea-fresh. He settled the helmet down over his head, hiding whatever feelings he might have.

Sir Nigel released his cloak, and it drifted out, over the horse's haunches. Sir Nigel accepted his helmet from my cold hands, the heavy iron bucket making a soft, dull chime as my fingers left it. He hefted the armored piece, like a market-day bargainer estimating the weight of a cheese. Now I heard myself saying what I believed could be my last words to my master.

"In Heaven's hands, my lord," I said, sounding as devout and calm as I wished I truly felt.

There had been a showy element to Sir Jean's kissing of the cross. Sir Nigel's prayer was almost silent, and reduced to two holy names.

"Our Lady and Saint George," said Sir Nigel.

The look he gave me was one of purest serenity, and something more.

Sir Nigel approached death as a famished man approaches a banquet. His arms were protected and strengthened by high-sleeved gauntlets, designed by Edmund. The gauntlet sleeves were fitted with splints of ashwood, provided by cutting up a spear and working it into the leather, the entire device strapped and bound into place. Sir Nigel had declared it the finest work since King David himself rode to battle.

My master felt the interior of the helmet, making sure the woolen head pad was in place, and while my hand lifted upward, following the helmet as it fitted down and over his head, I did not touch it now, letting Nigel make the adjustments that suited him.

I was sick at heart, certain I would never again see his face alive.

ELEVEN

A crowd of knights and their squires, as well as sailors and ship's boys, had gathered, a wide circle of folk.

The knights were hooded from the sun, the servants in flowing cloth caps of straw-brown homespun or once jaunty and now weathered colors. We were a battle-battered bunch. A few archers, jaundiced or heavily bandaged, sported the rounded leather caps of their kind. None of the Chian villagers had gathered. Even in a humming, welcoming port town, Crusaders had a reputation for unpredictable violence.

A farmer along a distant rocky path paused to let his donkey browse a stand of thistles and gazed down on us from the hillside. A line of clouds streaked down from the north, and despite the warm sun there was a harvest coolness in the light wind.

Sir Rannulf looked on, his eyes narrow, as though he

watched what was taking place from a great distance. Edmund watched quietly, appearing even taller than usual. Both Rannulf and Edmund were armed, Edmund carrying his gleaming war hammer. A joust sometimes began with two knights, attended by two sword-wielding squires, and then as events spilled out of control, fell into a general melee.

Edmund set aside his hammer and helped me strap on my simple brass and leather helmet, the chin buckle compressing my lips.

"Keep the sun at your back," said Rannulf.

Perhaps I should have been more forgiving, but Rannulf's advice annoyed me just then. He was a knight who could kill but could not battle, a cheerless, loveless fighting man who had won little glory on this Crusade. Besides, I thought, the joust would begin with the daylight against us, as anyone could see. The still climbing sun was behind Nicholas as that sturdily built squire adjusted his own head protection, a hooded coif of chain mail.

I felt envy and further anxiety. The hood fastened with a tie under Nicholas's chin and afforded him protection along his neck, and free movement. It gave a good appearance, too, and jingled softly as he shook his head to flex the armor, or show it off in the sunlight. No doubt, I tried to tell myself, the simple helmet I wore would protect against a blow almost as well.

Osbert took my arm. "Remember, my lord Hubert," he said, "they are liars and wretches." *Liyhers ant wrecches.* "Such men can never fight bravely."

I thanked him.

"And, Lord Hubert," said Osbert, in a confiding whisper,

"I hear Sir Jean cannot put his weight on both feet. If his horse spills, let Sir Jean try to stand up." He winked. "Sir Nigel will cut him to pieces, even with two broken arms."

I recalled the only joust I had ever witnessed, a tourney on a green outside Sheffield. The church disowned, and generally warned against, tournaments because they so often led to brutal homicides, spiteful knights dispatching old rivals. The Sheffield tourney, however, had promised blunted lances, and a lord mayor, chief burgess, or some other worthy had dropped a white flag to initiate the first of many breathtaking charges.

Clods had flown, and Sir William of Pontefract lost an eye, but wine had been drunk and rooks frightened. I recalled the black fowl clearly, perhaps what I could observe most successfully, being a boy among much taller city folk. The birds flew from nearby trees, settling again only to be frightened off once more, until after hours of broken lances and foaming chargers, the black birds at last had not bothered to stir a feather, and stayed where they were in the chestnut trees.

I folded Sir Nigel's cloak with great care. "Osbert says Sir Jean is weak-legged even now," I said.

"I can see that," said Nigel quietly. "But my thanks to you."

Sir Jean lowered his lance and lifted it, a brief salute. Sir Nigel responded with a gesture, a toss of his own lance, and then Sir Jean hulked forward, like a man about to topple from his horse.

He did not.

He leaned, and the warhorse carried him. The lance rose and fell, and then steadied as he came on.

TWELVE

Sir Nigel was not slow in kicking his horse, or hesitant in couching his lance, seating it under his elbow and leveling the weapon.

But Nereus the warhorse was not quick in responding. When the horse did react, he showed the wrong sort of spirit, tossing his head and snorting, the halter fittings jingling. Even when Nereus trotted forward, his ears were flattened, his eyes rolled, and he kicked out at nothing.

Sir Jean was already halfway across the field when Sir Nigel's voice, soothing and clucking, finally persuaded Nereus to barrel forward in the right direction. Sir Jean's lance shifted and searched as the knight rode forward, the point of the lance looking like a living, lethal creature.

Realizing that at the point of impact the two horsemen would not be approaching at equal speed, the cunning lance chose not to seek to impale Sir Nigel or drive him off the horse. The point hunted upward, toward that vulnerable seam in his armor, where the helmet and the chain mail left the throat exposed.

Horse furniture it is called, the breastplate and back plate of the saddle, girth and crupper of the leather, the snaffle bits of the harness. Every point of this furnishing strained as the lance point missed Sir Nigel's head, and the shaft of the lance caught Sir Nigel across the breast. Sir Nigel reeled, but did not haul at the reins or lurch in the saddle. He sat well, riding on through the point of impact as the lance levered out of Sir Jean's grasp and clattered to the dust.

I had a sudden, inappropriate thought: There, it's over and done, and now we can all feast and be friends.

It was far from done.

My own mount was trembling, shivers running along his frame, and it took only a touch of my spur knob to coax him forward. I rode hard through the dust in the air to Sir Nigel's struggling form, where he worked to wheel his horse around. At Nigel's side I tugged at his shield to straighten it—the strap had developed a twist. I helped him adjust his grip on the lance, neither of us speaking. As I turned to face Sir Jean and his squire, the sun was at our back.

Sir Jean kicked his mount, the force of the blow making the harness leap, and the charger was quick to respond. When the horse suddenly went down a moment later, it looked like an act of willfulness, the animal deciding to dump his knight and rest for a long moment on the ground.

The fall was so abrupt that even as I hauled at my reins,

slowing my approach, I had to puzzle together what I had seen and heard: the horse flinging his forward-striding hoof too high, a hind hoof stumbling, the whites of the animal's eyes wide and fearful. A loud, sickening snap.

The horse screamed, a sound not at all like a human cry, but one that nevertheless chilled me. Again the big animal cried, a full-lunged shriek. The horse flung out a foreleg, and the hoof angled straight down, swinging, connected only by flesh and sinew.

Sir Jean struggled to haul his body out of his saddle. It was no easy effort—one stirrup was trapped under the horse's heaving form. The saddle that helped the knight stay mounted and secure now trapped him. Nicholas held out a hand, leaning from his own mount, but Sir Jean slapped it away.

At last Sir Jean wrestled his bulk free of the horse. Nigel and I struggled to control our own chargers, both animals agitated by the agonized screams of the injured steed. Sir Jean drew his sword and in one blow cut his injured horse's neck, nearly all the way through.

One of Sir Jean's ostlers wailed, his voice high and broken as the sight of this fine horse bleeding moved him beyond words. Nearly every witness, many of them wagering men, had something solemn and urgent to say to his neighbors, and the air resounded with an undercurrent of voices.

Sir Jean used both hands to extricate the blade, pulling in a stiff, ugly movement, and then he brandished the weapon, gilded with blood. It was a gesture that both threatened and invited.

Sir Nigel laughed, his sound both captured and amplified

by the iron helmet. It was a single burst of merriment that from some fighters would have been empty bravado. But I knew Sir Nigel well enough. Mounted, Sir Jean, the bigger knight, had an advantage. But on foot, shield to sword, Sir Nigel could have traded blows with any warrior under heaven.

Unless he broke his arms again.

My own sword still in its scabbard, I held the leather bridle as Sir Nigel half fell from the saddle, caught himself, hefted his shield, and marched upon the larger knight, his chain mail skirt making the *chink chink chink* I found pleasant to hear under other circumstances.

A single bee, a spiraling speck of amber, circled crazily around Sir Nigel's helmet. The island of Chios was famed for its sage-flavored honey; from where we fought, straw beehives could be seen, a row upon the stony field. Sir Nigel hated insects and spiders, and even armored he hesitated now, letting this little chip of life make a wide orbit. Perhaps the bees mistook the blooming gush of scarlet all around for a sudden burst of flowers, because there were several insects, glinting brightly in the morning air.

Sir Nigel circled. Sir Jean set his feet and landed a sweeping blow on Sir Nigel's kite-shaped Crusader shield. In return Sir Nigel slammed his shield into Sir Jean's, shoving hard. I winced, looking on, knowing that if the splints and gauntlets protecting Sir Nigel were going to fail, it would be now.

"Pig!" grunted Sir Jean in English.

Pygge.

Sir Nigel cut through the air, his sword ringing out on the edge of Sir Jean's shield.

"Weak as a lady," said Sir Jean in his simple, infirm English. "Weak as a little maiden lady." *May-den lay-dee.*

Sir Nigel drove his shield into Sir Jean. The heavier Frankish knight took a step back and began to breathe heavily, his breath echoing in the iron bucket of his helmet.

"Thief master," panted Sir Jean.

I could not keep myself from stealing a glance at Squire Nicholas, wondering how embarrassing he found his lordship's invective. Nicholas allowed the mail coif to shadow his features.

Sir Nigel did not speak. The two knights circled each other. Sir Jean feinted once, twice. Sir Nigel, keeping his footwork economical, always thrust his left foot toward Sir Jean while the taller, stouter knight sometimes slipped, his feet confused, like a dancer too drunk to keep the tambour's rhythm.

"Piss hole!" gasped Sir Jean.

Sir Nigel delivered a solid, convincing blow squarely on the golden bird on Sir Jean's shield. Sir Jean shuffled, and his feet found the slop where the warhorse's gore had pooled. The big knight slipped. He stumbled, and caught himself only by sticking his sword into the scarlet muck.

Sir Nigel could have cut Sir Jean badly right then, the big knight exposed, but he did not. The Frankish fighting man staggered. He hopped on one foot, his mail skirt jingling, the sun bright along his polished shield. He swore by the Holy Face of Lucca, a favorite curse among knights.

And he fell hard, unharmed by Sir Nigel.

I was about to dismount. Nicholas's shadow was in the corner of my eye, his approach distorted by the sweat that stung my vision.

"Hubert!"

Edmund's voice.

I turned toward the movement rising near me—the gleam of a gauntlet, the glint of a sword.

But the sun was at my assailant's back.

With no warning, I was on the ground, flat, hands out, feet splayed, closing and opening my eyes. My ears were ringing, but I had no impression of having fallen. I was not concerned for the moment, and felt grateful for the flat, solid earth beneath me.

But as I lay there, I began to experience a deep puzzlement. Had I planned to do this? Surely, I mocked myself gently, this was not a good idea. I tried to imagine that the joust was over—it was time to stretch out in thankful exhaustion.

I had to guess my way through very recent events, and I found no logic behind my position here in the sunlight, men and horses moving about me, hooves kicking up dust. When I tried to sit up, I could not move.

Nicholas de Foss knelt over me, pressing my head down with one hand. The squire's mail coif whispered as he bent over me.

He lowered a *couteau*—a long knife—to my throat.

THIRTEEN

A fist seized the rounded top of Nicholas's coif and pulled him back.

Edmund had Nicholas, and as tall as the blond squire was, my friend raised him high off the ground and threw him down.

Edmund put the head of his war hammer on Nicholas's chest and said, "Do not move."

I parted my lips, but no words came.

"Where are your hurts?" asked Edmund, kneeling beside me.

"I am quite well, Edmund," I heard myself say—a perfect lie.

"Hubert, can you move?" Edmund insisted.

"When I choose," I managed to say.

A melee commenced, the field crowded with energetic, angry, impatient folk, excited to be battling again. Weapons made a terrible clash, shield against sword, hammer against armor. The sound makes the pit of the stomach leap, and the eyes blink. Mail-clad feet hurried around me, and the leather-bottomed boots of pikemen slipped in the bloody mud.

Edmund stood over me, laying about him with his hammer, warning people away. The tension was easily spent, and few men had drawn swords with murderous intent. Besides, this scurvy, jaundiced, worm-eaten crowd could not fight long without fatigue. Edmund stayed right where he was, one mailed foot on either side of me, keeping me from harm. Sir Nigel's voice rose over all the others. Just as in the Crusader camp, he won their attention, commanding men to sheathe their swords, and ordering squires to help their knights back to the tree shade where they could all drink cool wine.

Rannulf's voice reached me. In a calming tone he told some unseen warrior that if he did not scabbard his sword at once, he'd cleave his arm from his shoulder.

An ostler soothed one of the warhorses, with kissing sounds and quiet urging. A water boy outfitted in Sir Jean's worn and faded livery, a moth-eaten swift flying skyward on his breast, knelt beside Edmund.

"Sir Jean sends to know," said the lad, "if Sir Nigel's squire is badly hurt."

I tried to speak yet again, but could not form a further word. A great pain began to expand in my head.

"Good herald," said Edmund, his voice taut with anger, "pray ask Squire Nicholas's attendance upon us, if it please him."

———

Squire Nicholas wore his mail hood back, his blond hair sweat-soaked.

Edmund let the squire wait, wiping my face with a cool cloth. Then he stood and folded the cloth and made a show of bored surprise at Nicholas's presence. Edmund had learned a great deal among the Norman knights, and no one would have guessed he was a staver's son as he looked Nicholas up and down with nearly Frankish coolness.

"Upon my honor, Nicholas de Foss," said Edmund evenly, "and before Saint Mark, I swear that if I ever set eyes on you again I will take your life."

FOURTEEN

I had sometimes wondered how the trussed prize goose feels, carried from the market. I was trundled in Edmund's arms, with Rannulf marching ahead, the veteran knight only once having to call out, "Make way."

However, I was aware that if the pain in my head grew greater, I would die. And even as I struggled to be courageous, I felt the cold of this new fear seep into my bones. I promised myself that I would not lose consciousness or fall asleep.

I would stay awake forever.

I lay on a cot in our inn, and I slept, only to be shaken awake and offered a white, chipped bowl by Edmund. How he anticipated what I required I could not say, because I hardly knew myself. I disgorged the scanty contents of my belly, a brief bout of vomiting that left me feeling even weaker.

Edmund held my helmet into the lamplight so that I could see it. The head covering was cut badly, the brass and leather gashed. My head was sorely bruised, but as I searched with my fingers, it seemed that my scalp was intact.

The high-pitched shrilling in my ears was ceaseless, and I saw a double image of Sir Nigel as he entered the room.

Father Stephen, the English priest, paid me a visit, looking so wraithlike that I had to stretch out a hand and feel his arm through his sleeve.

"The weather has changed," said the priest.

I was not reassured by this visit, believing that I was sure to die and that this gaunt man of God was here to provide me with the appropriate rites. He did offer a few remarks on the sanctity of suffering, but then he sighed, and I realized— it had the force of fresh insight—that sometimes a priest needs comfort, too.

"It will be a blessing to see home again, Father," I offered, hoping he would allow me to adopt such a familiar tone.

"I dreamed of this," said the priest.

"You dreamed of what, Father?" I forced myself to ask.

"My parents were people of worth," said the priest. "With scullery servants and a bottler. But do you know, of all that luxury—" He let the word drift in the lamplight. Luxury was a sin, carnal and self-satisfying. "Of all that easeful luxury, do you know what I recall with the greatest joy?"

I could not shake my injured head.

"The sound of rain in the thatch," he rasped.

The priest and I shared the gentle sound of a downpour, increasing now beyond the shuttered windows.

A surgeon knelt before me, smelling of garlic and of sweat. He peered into my eyes, lifting my eyebrows as though he wanted my eyes to fall out so that he could examine them more completely. He put his hands over my head, fingertips pressing, as I cringed involuntarily. It did not hurt, I told myself.

Not very much.

He gestured to the crown of his own bald head. *"Cerebrum intacta est,"* he counseled in elemental, Greek-accented Latin. Sir Nigel and Edmund leaned forward expectantly in the lamplight. *"Ossae firmae,"* added the surgeon as though delivering good though unexpected tidings.

"He tells us you have a brain in your skull," said Sir Nigel, with the sort of forced cheer that good-hearted people use around the sick.

The surgeon turned down the corners of his mouth, and said something we were all free to interpret as *but his condition is not good*.

FIFTEEN

Surgeons dislike hale folk, preferring the ill. My mother cured illness by feeding us feverfew and valerian, and starving the fever out of our bodies.

And I, in turn, believe illness demands simple treatment, and dislike the guild of medical doctors. Besides, I doubt that surgeons know very much. Most doctors agree that the brain's function is to cool the blood. What I wanted to inquire was: Why, then, did a man always die if his brain was knocked out of his head?

But I did not argue with this foreign medical man. Instead I asked him politely, "How long will my head feel like a pail of river stones?"

Knowing he would not understand a word.

Osbert crept to my bedside, beaming. "We're all rich as millers again, my lord," he said.

I shaped the soundless question with my lips.

"I won a golden fibula brooch from a Norman squire," said Osbert, "and a blue jacinth-stone ring from his knight. The rest of the wager winnings were gold and silver." He offered me a piece of apple, from a fruit he was carving with a short blade. "A Norman apple," he said. "Beyond price—almost."

I thanked him for the piece of fruit, which, although mealy with age, was sweet enough. "Do knights agree," I asked, "that Sir Nigel was the victor?" In my judgment, neither knight had won a clear triumph.

"Can you doubt it, my lord? Besides, I wagered that Sir Nigel would be standing at the end of the joust, nothing more. Only Norman fighting men would take the bet, although they made up for their numbers in foolishness."

"This is good fortune for you," I said, nearly mistaking the sound of my voice for that of a very old man. "But it brings no coin into my purse."

"Oh, I borrowed from what remained of your silver, my lord, both you and Edmund. I placed a wager here and there, with honest men. You are as rich as ever you were." He made his eyes wide with enthusiasm, and put a hand on my bedding. "And I won back your excellent thimble from a servant of Sir Jean's, and that noble drinking cup of Edmund's, too."

I felt drowsy, but I could hear him say, "Only don't tell Sir Nigel, good Hubert. I fear he dislikes a gambler."

I stirred, and sat up to call after him, but my head throbbed as Osbert faded out of the lamplight.

I was carried by Edmund onto the *Santa Croce,* bound for Genoa. Edmund placed me gently into a sling, a hanging sailcloth bed in the freshly scrubbed, vinegar-scented hull of this vessel.

From above drifted the thuds and curses of someone being beaten. I have always disliked beatings, whether of man or brute, and I was heartsick at the sound of this captain or ranking mate belaboring a sailor with what sounded like a rope end.

The beating stopped at last. Sir Jean and Nicholas were aboard another galley, one that had already left, bound for Malta or Crete—Edmund was not sure which. It was fairly certain that the Frankish knight and his English squire would find swift transportation to Paris or London. "Sir Nigel would rather sail with a load of lepers than with Sir Jean and Nicholas," Edmund said. It was expected that Nicholas would reach London before us.

"Besides," I said, "if you see Nicholas, you'll have to kill him."

"I will have his life," said Edmund, "as I have sworn." He spoke as one who would not be moved, and using a diction a little foreign to both of us, law-bound and formal.

"Was that, do you think, Edmund, the wisest oath to make?"

The vibration of my own voice caused me pain. Although

suffering is a gift from Heaven, as the English priest had reminded me—allowing us to experience a tiny portion of Our Lord's suffering—I did not consider myself particularly blessed.

"I have made the oath," said Edmund. "I cannot unsay it."

My mother and my father were prayerful, and paid Father Giles good coin to teach me Latin verbs, but my mother once said, "Strong piety is for the priest, Hubert, and not for folk like us, who sup on white bread and the best peas." My parents gave alms, and treated every soul with courtesy, but felt that God and the saints were not closely connected with a well-spoken woolman's life.

Many fighting men were both far more brutal and more devout than I. But even I recognized that a sacred oath, made while touching a holy relic—a saint's bone or a reliquary of saint's hair—was a contract with God. So was an oath invoking a holy name or divine entity, like Heaven. And an oath upon one's honor placed one's reputation, future and past, at stake.

I said, "Knights should call you Edmund Stronghead."

He laughed gently.

Only later, much later, when the other squires had attached their canvas beds to hooks in the ship's timbers, and the keel rose and fell, did I wake, brimming over with a warning.

I tried to climb out of my swinging bed.

"Stay easy," said Rannulf's voice. He pressed a clay bottle

to my lips, and I drank poppy wine. It was a thick, sweet medicine, with a tarry undertaste.

For a taciturn man, Sir Rannulf was a tireless nurse, and had sat with Edmund during our voyage to the Holy Land when fever robbed my friend of strength and reason. I had begun to wonder if the seasoned knight had his own species of mercy.

"You should have seen the blow coming," Rannulf chided gently. "Always be ready to check the blade," he added, offering perhaps the oldest rule in swordplay.

But before I could make a sound, the poppy wine snuffed all thought, even as I struggled against it.

Don't trust him, I wanted to say.

Don't trust Osbert.

SIXTEEN

The ship's captain was called Giorgio al Cimino, broad and bowlegged, a man not too proud to call on me in my sickbed, as I swung to the movement of the sea.

He swore by his name saint, the patron of warriors, the famous dragon slayer. He gave my friends Genoan-sounding names, *Nigello, Ranolfo, Edmundo.* He said that he was proud to have us all on his ship.

Captain Giorgio swung a knotted rope, judging by the sound, although he varied his choice of instruments, sometimes using a tawse, a leather strap that made a fine cracking noise against the deck. For long hours I could judge his position on the ship by his thumping blows. In my dazed state I believed I could hear demonic voices—or, perhaps, goats.

Father Stephen visited me again, and reminisced about his boyhood pleasures. He said that his family had enjoyed the services of a cupboard, supplied "floor to roof beam with meat pies. Pigeon, both cock and squab. And pullet and cockerel, and every venison pie known to man. We ate such on meat days, of course," meaning that his family went meatless on Fridays, as the Church decreed. "And mead," he recalled, entranced at the memory. "We drank mead at table, not brown ale."

I let him describe these early days, feeling that Father Stephen was weaker than ever and sustained by the memory of comforts he might never taste again.

As an afterthought, he turned back to me one evening and said, "Squire Hubert, you have lost the look of a young man about to die. Unless pirates intercept us, of course. Then—" He ran a quaking finger across his throat.

Pyratys.

The word sounded familiar, but I could not guess its meaning.

"Thieves," he said in his thin, unsteady voice, "of the sea!"

Some people have praised the power of the poppy drug, sap from a blossom that flourishes in the distant East. Mixed with tart red wine to disguise the bitter flavor, it erases pain and delights the soul with dreams.

Or so I had been told. My poppy visions were tediously detailed—a splendid tower house, a castle assembled stone by stone. I beheld such a building take shape in my waking dreams, constructed by invisible masons, with oak roof beams, a strong tower for defense, a solar room for quiet moments, turrets, newel staircases, one wardrobe for garments, and another for armor. There was an audience chamber—surely this was a house for a bishop—and traceried windows, richness I had never actually seen in life.

At last, aching for fresh air, I rolled from my sailcloth swing, and groped for the ladder.

The sea dash cleared my head. The air tasted of salt, and of salt fish, and something pungent and earthy.

A goat pen was crowded with animals, nannies and young billies. The captain cracked a lash, hitting nothing.

I observed to Edmund, "He isn't very accurate with his blows, is he?"

Edmund turned, surprised.

"I am not Lazarus," I said, laughing weakly, "risen from a hole in the ground."

"You are thin enough to be a corpse," said Edmund with a smile. "But don't worry—we'll fatten you."

Osbert sidled up to me and said, "I never had any doubt of your recovery, good Hubert."

I eyed Osbert with the keenest interest.

"I have wagered," said the servant, "that we'll be on the Rhône River by Saint Andrew's day."

The feast day for that first of Christ's apostles is at the end of November, which meant we had some weeks of sailing yet. The Rhône is a Frankish river, one of several possible routes north to England. Autumn was well in force here at sea, cold wind bellying the *Santa Croce*'s sails. For a painful moment I ached for home, my father stamping his feet as he came in off Fisher Street with a song on his lips.

I found myself taking heart at Osbert's description of the fishing vessels we had passed, not one of them fast enough to keep up with the *Santa Croce*.

"Slow as the last flies of summer, my lords," Osbert was saying.

"And no sign," I asked hopefully, "of pirates?"

"No pirate would attempt a ship like ours, good Hubert," said Osbert, "bristling with swords."

"Look here—Osbert mended your helmet," said Edmund.

I ran my fingers over the neat stitches.

"I didn't know you had so many skills," I said.

"I have many ways of serving two worthy squires," said Osbert. "And I can mend my ways as well as I can stitch leather."

"Can you?" I asked.

"By my faith," said Osbert, sounding like any reformed sinner.

Because I thought that I was mistaken about Osbert—or because I believed that the crafty servant had changed his ways—I did not voice my fears.

All went well for days.

The chilly wind drove us into swells, and soaked us if we lingered in the bow. But we dined on boiled goat and goat cheese, and drank pitchers of amber wine. My head no longer hurt. Sir Nigel responded to my question about sea thieves by saying that Osbert was right—any right-minded pirate would fly from us. "We're the most fearsome ship on this sea."

The assortment of ailing and injured knights and squires became less like aggrieved Crusaders, forced by ill luck to leave the Holy Land, and more like travelers beginning to envision the cooking smoke and friendly smiles of far-off home.

Sir Nigel was strong enough now to unsheathe his sword and make it ring against a practice shield, a battered, cut-up target. I held up the shield, dancing with the shifting of our vessel, until my own arms began to ache. Then Edmund braced his feet and gave Sir Nigel something of a contest, feinting with the target, dodging, making a rough game of it, Sir Nigel laughing with satisfaction.

It was not the first time that I believed Edmund was destined to be a better fighter than I would ever be, once he learned to use footwork and timing, and to wield the sword like an artful weapon and not like a club. Sir Rannulf folded his arms and smiled with evident pleasure at the sight of Sir Nigel's return to strength, and the other knights looked on indulgently and called out good-natured mockery. But some of the sailors went pale at the smash and bang of this sword practice, especially when Sir Nigel and Sir Rannulf let their naked steel swords ring against each other, brisk and dangerous sport on a coursing ship.

Captain Giorgio showed his white teeth and coiled his knotted rope, but the sailors were tight-lipped, aware, I thought, that they were outnumbered if a crew of swordsmen decided to take the ship to some closer port than far-off Genoa. "We wouldn't dream of such a thing," said Edmund when I mentioned this.

He considered a moment longer. "Would we?"

I woke often at night to the groaning of the ship, the sea hissing as we sped before the wind, and I could not tell if the cry I had just heard was one of our dwindling number of nanny goats, or something human.

When I heard the squabbling voices that morning, I was not surprised. Perhaps some Crusader had in fact decided to threaten the crew into making for a nearby port.

Some trouble had been steeping all this while, but as I climbed into the sunlight behind Edmund, I stopped in my tracks.

Captain Giorgio held Osbert to the deck.

SEVENTEEN

Osbert protested, "I have done nothing."

A sailor held up a purse, a leather money pouch, with a gash along the seam. He held up a short blade, too, the sort of sharp kitchen knife that is carried in the pocket with the point buried in a ball of wax.

I had seen this knife in Osbert's hand just days before, cutting an apple.

"My lords, I am guiltless," piped Osbert.

"Edmund, bring my sword," said Nigel.

"I'll do it," said Edmund.

Sir Nigel turned to look at him.

"He's my servant," said Edmund, "brought by me from the battlefield. I'll punish him myself."

Sir Nigel said, in a low voice, confiding and gentle, "You know what the punishment has to be?"

Osbert gave out a high, crystalline wail, a keen sound that startled all of us into silence.

"No, good Edmund," said Osbert at last. "Let Sir Nigel cut me, please—not you."

Edmund was gone, down into the hull. He returned with a sword in its black leather scabbard. He drew Sir Nigel's blade, and looked to me without speaking.

Rannulf and I seized Osbert, and were in the act of stretching out the servant's arm against the deck when Osbert shifted, contracted his body, and forced it into a ball. Exasperated, Rannulf and I reached to grapple with him.

Osbert sprang up and leaped onto the rail as a flume of spray streaked through the morning sun. He jumped.

For an instant his head bobbed in the lacy foam of our wake.

And then he vanished.

EIGHTEEN

We never saw him again.

In the hours following Osbert's death, Edmund watched the sea. He peered into the ship's wake, hurried from one rail to the other, and climbed to the limit of the bow, seeking a glimpse of his servant. At last he returned to the stern again, his head cocked, as though listening for Osbert's voice, still expecting to see his face appearing out of the wind-scored swells.

I joined him there beside the helmsman, a man tanned and wrinkled by the sun. Sir Nigel arrived to mark Edmund's mood, and took the opportunity to remark on the distant islands.

"Greek strongholds," he said, to distract Edmund from his mourning. "Some of them were visited by the great knight Ulysses himself, in his legendary travels."

"Ulysses sailed home through these waters?" I asked.

"Certainly," said Nigel, eager to distract Edmund with any sort of conversation. "And had his men turned into breed-boars by a famous witch. Although," he added with a chuckle, "I believe many sailors are half pig already."

The wind was powerful and swept us onward, each fling of spray stinging our eyes. Sailors had searched the thin bedroll and cracked leather satchel, all of Osbert's remaining possessions. Squires and knights alike exclaimed at the rings and brooches that appeared, small objects of value that their owners had thought lost or mislaid.

"Osbert had my trust," said Edmund, interrupting our attempts to entertain him with talk. *Mi truste.*

"And mine," I offered, but Edmund would only give me a pained smile.

"Leave him to the saints," said Sir Nigel.

I wondered what the Heavenly Host would make of our bright-eyed, lively servant, and whether Our Lord would forgive him for his quick, too-clever hands.

The *Santa Croce* had one of the old-fashioned steerboards, not a rudder but an oarlike device unattached to the stern. Edmund offered to help the helmsman, and his assistance was accepted as Nigel and I looked on.

Edmund's eyes took on a sorrowful serenity as he guided the ship, the helmsman—a stout individual with many missing teeth—beside him offering quiet encouragement in a half-comprehensible dialect.

"I think," said Nigel, "our friend Edmund is a born seaman."

———

Our ship began to show signs of wear.

Water began to slosh back and forth in the hold, and two men worked a pump during daylight hours, in an effort to preserve the rummage, the casks and chests stored there. The pump was a wheezing, spluttering mechanism, a bellowslike affair. The sailors showed every evidence of urgency, and they sang holy songs as they worked.

Sir Nigel tried to coax our priest, but, after a day of brooding, Father Stephen continued to maintain that no soul dead by suicide deserved even a brief shipboard rite, and certainly not Osbert. Sir Nigel at last called a short requiem into the salt spray, and one of the Genoan sailors gave prayer in his vernacular, a common port language, unfit for holy office. It was the language of taverns and dice cups, and yet when the prayer spoke of Dio, more than one of us made the sign of the holy cross.

Afterward Sir Nigel confided to me that "ship men are a devil-fearing lot. That's why we need the prayers, to lay the ghost."

"Do ghosts pursue Genoans in particular?" I asked, trying to make light of the subject.

"What man doesn't fear the devil?" said Sir Nigel.

Early one predawn, the spruce-wood mast split, with a resounding report.

Captain Giorgio adopted the habit of actually striking his sailors with the knotted rope he swung, and the ship took on a glum, harried atmosphere, passengers and crew alike watching the weather and the distant rise and fall of land. To take the pressure off the mast, sails were set on stays that thrust out on either side of the ship, so that our vessel must have looked like some great, oceangoing hen.

The water in the bilge sloshed and groaned with a sound like Osbert's *my lord, my lords,* and at night I woke, sure that I had heard the servant whisper, *Soon, my lord Hubert.*

You'll swim with me soon.

They call it *rak,* the scudding, low clouds that crawl across the sky. Some folk can read the shapes of clouds and see the harm to come. My father said such talk was foolish, but paid good coin to a stargazer once to hear my future told.

The astrologer recorded the hour of my birth, scratching the details onto vellum with a new goose quill. "Taurus," he intoned meditatively, studying the scroll, "with Gemini rising. A nature that contradicts itself. Brave at heart, but changeable. Well-liked, but determined."

"That's my Hubert!" said my father.

A week later the cunning man invited my father and the younger, boyish version of myself into his smoky study. "Your son will do you honor," he said, smiling within his scholar's beard. "He will be a pilgrim, according to the stars."

My father leaned forward in his chair. He had hoped to learn that I was destined for knighthood, and could not hide his disappointment.

"He'll travel to many holy shrines," said the astrologer hastily. "He'll win you the favor of Heaven with his prayers."

My father had paid good silver for the best sword masters he could hire, and swore ever after that astrologers were fools.

Now I wished I had the advice of a wise, far-seeing fortune-teller. The ship was surrounded by rising mist that twisted into shapes like ghosts, and when a sailor spoke, the words died on his lips, every sound absorbed by the chilly vapor.

ΠΙΠΕΤΕΕΠ

Land appeared again one afternoon, a rind of coast, low and featureless. Captain Giorgio poured a cup of red wine from the goatskin he kept near the mast, and lifted it in salute to the far-off coast.

"Italia!" he exclaimed.

My heart quickened.

Somewhere on that landscape ruled the lord pope. The city of Rome, the capital of Christendom, with its myriad holy sites, was shielded by distance and sea haze from our hungry eyes. After Jerusalem, Rome was the most sacred city in the world. Every Christian dreamed of a pilgrimage to its holy places. The chains Saint Peter had worn in prison were kept in Rome, and the city boasted the magnificent and hideous Colosseum of legend, where holy martyrs had suffered lions to eat their still-living flesh, to the glory of God.

The wind had been bitter but strong, driving us under a clear sky. As we bucked the swells and began our journey north, along the long stretch of Italian mainland, the sky was rutted with cloud. The moon winked and vanished behind this scudding gray, and the sun rose scarlet and oval, giving no heat and little light.

Soon, soon, said a guttering whisper.

The ship wallowed, shrugged off rushing waves, and then leaned into them, bobbing away from the sea, turning into it—trying every tactic, like a weary swordsman, to endure the pounding water.

I took heart at the crashing foam, and Edmund smiled through the sling stones of water. It was harsh weather, but this was, after all, an adventure. The storm drove every other thought, and every sorrow, from our souls. We were happy again, in our ignorance of the ways of the sea. We had faith in the mariners, and in the ship.

The sailors worried the rigging, and used heavy wooden mauls to drive stops—canvas wadding—into gaps where the ship's timbers began to part.

TWENTY

We ran aground one morning.

Sailors swore by Our Lady, and we all breathed prayers of our own, but the captain swung his knotted rope, cried out orders with the air of a man who was unconcerned. He caught my eye and called through the whistling rain something about land and sea and ships, how no one could predict a storm.

But as the day wore on, the vessel began to labor, stuck fast to the bottom. The captain, no longer putting on even a demonstration of calm, drove his men with a long ox whip. Men in the hold called out, straining and gasping, frantically working the pumps.

Rannulf made his way through the rushing foam. "The ship is breaking up," he said.

"Do you believe so?" asked Sir Nigel. He cocked his head. "Yes, you may be right, Rannulf, by my faith."

Sir Nigel and Sir Rannulf talked about ships, taking turns speaking loudly into each other's ears against the shriek of the wind. They agreed that even the strongest oak beam can take a downward force more successfully than a weight from the side. Speaking as though they had hours to analyze and compare, they admired the Genoans' vigor, but agreed that the captain had more bluster than ability.

Years of war study, planning siege engines and catapults, and finding out through experience which lances shatter and which can endure, gave them a midwife's calm eye for trouble. Edmund and I clung to ropes, and at last I cried out, "What can we do?"

"Do?" Sir Nigel gave one of his manly, exasperating laughs, perhaps joking at his own tough-mindedness. "If Heaven calls us, we'll go."

Rannulf was drenched, rain and brine streaming from his beard. "Go get our war-kits and our safe-chest, both of you. Hurry!"

The hold stank.

The sour odor of dank cheeses, smoked fish, and moldy biscuit rose around us from the black water. Sergeants and squires elbowed, scrambling in the near dark. Sailors cursed; two men came to blows. Other knights had given the same command, it seemed. Body was wedged against body, but with a willed patience, most squires manhandled their masters' war gear up and out of the hold without bloodshed.

———

At midday sailors jumped down into the seething surf and began to unload the ship into tenders, ship-to-shore boats that bobbed and spun in the water. The surf was just shallow enough to allow a tall man to stand with his nose and mouth out of the water. When the keel snapped, with a single, heart-stopping crash, a few squires tumbled overboard in a panic. One head bobbed and vanished, and other squires strained to reach a tender and cling to its side.

We abandoned the *Santa Croce.*

Despite the shallow waters, we were far from shore, but we could struggle forward along the sandy bottom, holding our equipment over our heads. Other knights and squires joined us, with an air of resigned necessity rather than panic. Our equipment was lashed together, swords and mail attached to our chest of treasures. One squire sang out a chant of praise to Our Lady, but when we were well away from the protective bulk of the ship, and the surf began to cut our legs out from under us, voices began to sputter and call for help.

I swallowed bitter salt water, inhaled it, coughed it up. I could not see the shoreline, but I made out Edmund's voice, calling for Sir Nigel.

I heard no answering cry.

TWENTY-ONE

The water lifted me and flung me forward, jamming my face into the sandy shore.

The first drowned man I pulled from the surf was Father Stephen.

I dragged several more bodies, bawling into the hard wind for Sir Nigel and Edmund. Sir Rannulf labored with me, hauling sodden men out of the boiling foam, and soon a line of drenched figures sprawled above the waterline. Some crawled or struggled to roll over and put their faces to the rain. Others remained inert, in postures that can only be adopted by the lifeless, arms entangled, mouths agape.

Edmund called my name, dragging a drenched figure from the sea. A sharp wave nearly spilled him, and he flung the body over his shoulders like a meal sack. I recognized Sir Nigel's short, silver hair.

The knight's arms dangled as Edmund kicked free of the foam. He flung the knight down hard, and stood helplessly over his body. Then he seized Sir Nigel's ankles and held him up like a life-size poppet, a child's play figure. He shook the knight, and a long gush of water spouted from Sir Nigel's mouth. The knight waved his arms, swung a fist, cried out something, and Edmund stretched him out on the sand.

All along the line of bodies, women and children had appeared from inland, the wind fluttering shawls and blouses as they stooped over the sprawling drowned and half-drowned. This was proof that in this unknown countryside some welcome would be provided—food, a warm hearth. But as I staggered up the wet sand to offer my greetings, I glimpsed the flash of a knife.

These were scavengers, cutting corpses of their purses, buckles, rings—and if a body was still coughing, a quick in-and-out quieted all complaint. I cursed a shawled figure, swung a fist and missed, and she raised a high, sharp cry.

Several shadows that had been watching from a copse of stunted pines left their hiding and hurried down the sandy beach armed with cudgels and staves. I had studied sword work with scarred sergeants, the best fighters my father could afford. I am not easily frightened by an attack, but unarmed as I was now, I took a few blows on my forearms before I began to fight successfully with my fists.

My attacker was a farmer, judging by his beige-cloth apron and tunic, and although his cap was cut in a style I did not recognize, I saw in him a harvester's strength, broad feet, heavy forearms. Such men have long ago mastered the downward stroke, splitting the ox skull with a single blow. I avoided his heavy swings, bloodied his face, knocked him down, and kicked him until he was still. Then I dealt with his fellow farmers, joined by Edmund, who was also unarmed but lost no time in snatching a truncheon, breaking it over a head, and driving another assailant into the sand.

Sir Rannulf's opponent leaped at him with a knife. It is one of the earliest lessons in combat, how to knock aside a thrust and step inside your opponent's guard. Sir Rannulf half killed the farmer with a blow to his face, and seized the knife from his stunned grasp. The knight knelt over his attacker and, taking a swine butcher's care, cut his throat.

All the scavengers fled, bleeding, staggering, except Rannulf's dying man, the dark red spreading in the sand around him.

When several new figures stood on a ridge, observing us from a height, we gathered together. One of the hooded men was on horseback, and all of them carried staffs. We had no weapons, and our company was small: a few coughing, spewing sailors, some half-dazed Frankish squires, and the four of us.

"We must live to see Rome," rasped Sir Nigel.

Rannulf retrieved the knife from the dead man's throat, and Edmund dug a scrap of timber from the foam, a piece of flotsam from the *Santa Croce*. The ship was broken-backed beyond the surf, a dark, fragile husk. Edmund brandished the improvised club, took a swipe at the air, and then motioned to the far-off men, *Come on*.

I had to love Edmund's spirit. I wrapped a length of wet cordage around my fist. My friend and I would not die easily. The figures on the ridge fanned out, the horsemen directing them, hoods and mantles billowing in the wind. They were calling as they approached, a foreign curse or battle cry.

TWENTY·TWO

Only when they were close enough for us to see their eyes did we notice the crosses dangling around their necks, and the wine sack held aloft. The unarmed men slowed as they approached.

"Sheathe your weapons, men," said Sir Nigel with something like humor.

Edmund let the wooden club fall and sank to his knees, exhausted.

The hearth fire danced in the center of the hall.

We drank spiced wine, the hot drink doing little to dissolve the lingering cold in my feet, my joints, along the long muscles of my back. I huddled in a coarse blanket as holy brothers, members of a devout order, set wooden platters with slabs of bread and cheese before us. The other survivors were warmly attended as well, one or two of them close to death.

"I pray to every saint," said Sir Nigel, "that I never set foot on a ship as long as I live."

I considered before I spoke. "Will you not return to England?"

"We have been spared for a high purpose," Nigel said, ignoring the question.

"If Heaven desires that we travel by sea—" I continued.

"Then, yes, I'll hire myself out as a helmsman," snapped Sir Nigel, with a welcome hint of his old spirit.

There is warm hospitality in the company of such monks. My father and I had stayed in an inn run by an abbey—the Mitre and Sword—when we traveled to Derby. We had some casual friends among the clergy, who saved their best ale for us—or so they led us to believe—in a pitcher on the top shelf.

But because such people have devoted their lives to Our Lord, they offer all travelers the same benevolent care. I think there is something impersonal in the mercy of someone who does not know my name, but this is no doubt because of the smallness of my own soul, when matched with those who serve God. I was grateful that night to hear the rain spitting on the fire from the smoke hole in the roof.

I used my Latin to ask one of the brothers how far we were from Rome, and he said we were less than ten leagues from that city.

"Ten leagues!" I exclaimed, repeating the news to Sir Nigel.

"How far is that?" asked Sir Nigel.

I was momentarily crestfallen at my own ignorance. "It can't be far."

"Far or long," said Nigel, "we'll find King Richard's ambassador to Rome, and make ourselves useful to him."

The Crusade had not changed Nigel the way woad dye turns raw wool to blue. But some new stitchery was present in the fabric of his character, a new quiet. I hoped this meant that Sir Nigel foresaw a long, safe life ahead, and not that he expected to die soon and desired a conscience full of grace.

"We are poor now, all of us," said Sir Rannulf, cutting off another slice of brown bread, and offering it around before taking a bite himself. Perhaps Rannulf had changed recently, too, I thought, although I could not measure his moods and silences so easily. Certainly he had been a friend to me in my illness, but I was not sure I could trust a man who cut a throat as unemotionally as he sliced a loaf.

"The treasure will wash up on the shore," I said.

"No iron floats, nor any gold," said Edmund solemnly.

All of our armor, our silver—my thimble, Edmund's cup. In my gratitude at being alive, I had not felt the loss until now.

"Surely we'll find something," I said.

"We're as wealthy as a gang of tomcats," said Sir Nigel, with a matter-of-fact good humor. "No more, and no less." Poverty was not a shameful condition—some chose that state, seeking to work in almshouses among the ill, or to travel on endless pilgrimage to holy places. But for a pair of squires looking to establish themselves as knights, our loss was devastating.

———

I left the smoky hall and its candlelight, and walked out into the sheltered corridor, the rain visible through a row of arches. I blinked angry tears, and I made no move to hide them when Edmund joined me, looking at the dark rainfall.

"Sir Nigel," I said, "has an honorable name, even if he is as poor as a billy goat. What do we have?"

Edmund had been born to a man who carved barrel staves, a man for whom three or four silver pennies a year would have been remarkable bounty. Poverty suited him—he had his strength and his good sense. My father had money, but the sort of wealth that winds up invested in contracts with dyers and warehouses. He had borrowed against shiploads of woven wool bound for Brugge and paid for my gauntlets and my sword, both he and my mother drinking watered wine to afford a son who might someday be knighted.

"It's all lost," said Edmund, with a calm seriousness.

"This is not the way to spread joy, Edmund. 'It's all lost,'" I intoned, sounding exactly like him.

"We have our lives," he said huskily.

He was right, of course.

He added, "I shall miss my hammer."

At once, I felt ashamed. I had been pitying myself for the loss of my imagined future, and my friend had suffered a painful loss, the hammer Rannulf had given him.

I prayed silently to Saint Michael that two squires not be forgotten. And I continued to believe that some portion of our treasure might be recovered.

———————

I slept badly, dreaming of leather purses unseamed and spilling, gold-framed brooches blistered with sea life, fish nosing the long, keen blades of swords.

The beach was wide and nearly empty of life in the dawn.

The *Santa Croce* was reduced to a few ribs and the stump of a mast, so far off from the shore that I was astonished we could have struggled to safety.

The sand was cluttered with rope and pegs, broken kegs, wrecked casks, the angle of a doorjamb, a bundle of headless arrow shafts—and naked corpses, pale in the sea foam. A few scavenger folk scampered up the beach at our approach, and watched as we hauled the human remains, fish-gnawed, cold, and stiff, up to the dry slope.

We stumbled over rolls of cordage, broken wooden hogsheads for ale, butt ends from wine barrels, but nothing gold, nothing silver, and no weapons. When Rannulf braved the gray seas in a boat, a pair of strong-armed monks to row, he searched the far-off hull, clinging like a crab. He held up his few finds—a mail mitten, leather legging, a shield—but cast them down again.

At last he returned to shore with the air of a man who had done everything he could.

The scavengers watched from a ridge. One of them raised a defiant weapon, a club—or was it a sword? There were more of them now. These were not the shabby figures of the day before, but bulky, hooded field men, expert treasure seekers.

The scavengers rose and retreated as I ran toward them.

But some of them looked back, beckoning with brazen cheers.

Rannulf seized me from behind and threw me to the sand.

"They have our swords!" I protested.

Rannulf shook his head, breathing hard.

"And they have our silver!" I said.

"What little they have," he said, "let them keep."

I turned my face into the sea wind, and it was a long time before I spoke again.

TWENTY-THREE

We carried staffs, and we needed them.

The farmland we traveled through was clean-swept by the recent rains. Puddles gleamed under the sky, and heavy-jowled dogs were loosed on us by distant peasants. Rannulf drove the beasts away with ease, stabbing the animals harmlessly but painfully with the end of his strong staff, digging into each cur's snarl until no dog was fierce enough to do more than bark canine oaths after us.

We were dressed now in the simple rough-woven wool of pilgrims, with cowls and full sleeves. Even a duke or royal steward on a pilgrimage to Rome wore such a costume, and there was honor in simplicity. Still, I regretted not resembling a knight's squire—I cut a certain figure when I wear a weapon.

A group of armed men watched us at a crossroads, wearing swords and light shields, the sort called targets, round and easy to carry. These youths were unhelmeted and tanned by the sun. They commented on us as we passed, words of no meaning to my ears but perfectly understandable nonetheless—assertions regarding our character, our parentage, our fighting spirit.

Sir Rannulf marched ahead, his pilgrim garb failing to disguise his determined stride or the way he carried the staff like a weapon.

A stone bounded beside us, followed by a laugh from behind.

"Five of them, all armed, one with a two-handed sword," said Nigel, as though he was seriously contemplating our chances.

Another stone hummed past, white, the size of a robin's egg. It barely missed Edmund's head.

I plucked the missile from the road.

"What will you do with that?" asked Nigel.

"I can hit a magpie at fifty paces," I asserted.

"And hurt it," Edmund asked, "or merely startle the bird out of its feathers?"

"And stop it dead," I said.

This was an exaggeration. I used to visit my father's shepherds, and magpies were a grievous nuisance to lambs. Sometimes, I had been told, they pecked out a young animal's eyes—many shepherds used slings to protect their herds. The sound of a leather sling whirring was enough to send the crafty black-and-white fowl into the trees and safety. Although I never mastered the sling, I had hit a few of the birds, throwing bare-handed.

I think I stunned one, in years of trying.

"I'll hit one of those churls between the eyes," I asserted. A churl was a field man of little rank.

"I doubt you can," said Sir Nigel.

I threw wide of the loudest mischief maker, and he hurled the stone back so hard it whistled. Edmund and I made a desultory game of finding appropriate stones on the road, tossing them in our hands, and, when a stone was the right size and heft, throwing it at our ragtag opponents. At last I came close, making the tallest one duck.

Rannulf wandered back to join in the sport, and he succeeded, on his second try, in striking a rotund youth in the belly. The young man called out something equivalent to *It didn't hurt a bit,* but with this easy success Rannulf became less interested in the game.

"There's no honor in bruising villeins," he explained, striding on ahead of us again.

A villein was a peasant whose entire laboring life was owned by a lord. Many knights held such folk to be little better than livestock, but it was not the first time that I had wondered at Rannulf's dry nature. Edmund and I had speculated on his dislike for women, and his leathery manner toward people in general.

Edmund had wondered if the cruel scar across Rannulf's mouth—giving him a permanent, silent snarl—had made Rannulf bitter toward humanity, to protect himself from having his overtures of friendliness rebuffed. I disagreed with my friend. I believed simply that some folk are bitter and dangerous, and that—despite his occasional kindness—Rannulf was one of them.

The taunts of the field men followed us, and became a

sort of rude companionship, until we left them far behind. The farmland was bare and flat under the clear sky. Tall straight trees aimed in green rows toward Heaven. Short stone towers overlooked harvest stubble. Green pines, with rounded tops like oaks, shaded the road. There were kind souls along the road—a woman who gave us cups of warm, foaming cow's milk, a plowman who broke off handfuls of golden bread. Children skipped to the edge of the way and offered us curious smiles.

When we reached a paved high road, Sir Nigel noted that the wide paving stones were scored by the passage of carts. "Many heavy wagons, is my guess," he said, "over many years."

Father Giles had visited Rome, and said it was scarred with evidence of the empire-building pagans who had lived there. "Iron-wheeled chariots," I suggested.

The domes of time-pocked buildings approached us along the road. "These are the burial sites," I hazarded, recalling what I could of Father Giles's accounts, "of famous Roman knights."

"They buried their men-at-arms in temples?" queried Edmund.

"Like any people of good sense," said Nigel, "the Caesars, no doubt, were a ghost-respecting lot."

Before Edmund and I could absorb this, Rannulf's voice reached us, calling with an uncharacteristic emotion.

———

"Look!"

It was the first time I had heard the knight sound so excited.

The shoulders of monuments, the belfries of sacred places clustered in the distance behind city walls. Bells sounded, the music softened by the miles we had yet to travel, and the tumult of a great city pattered and rang through the sunlight.

TWENTY-FOUR

"It would take ten thousand men to storm these walls," said Rannulf, wonder in his voice.

The red clay-stone walls rose above us, and a city gate studded with iron. The gate had closed before us at our approach.

"And then you would have a street battle," Rannulf continued to muse. "Nearly always a pikeman's fight, not a knight's."

"We will enter like lambs," said Sir Nigel.

I made the sign of the cross, in part to show my earnestness as a Christian knight, and partly to steady my will. Guards armed with halberds and broad-brimmed helmets looked down at us from the top of the wall. Knights rarely engaged personally in an initial parley—announcements of name and rank were generally made through a chief squire. This saved a knight any hint of disrespect or insult while his identity and intentions were established.

"We are Crusaders," I called upward, "just returned, with news of King Richard of the English and King Philip of the Franks."

Two armored heads looked down at me, with no sign of understanding.

I spoke in English, in Latin, and in Norman-Frankish. I was about to invent a language on the spot, half gesture and half shipboard Genoan, when I heard one of the guards say, among other words, *Crociato,* conferring with his fellows.

"Si!" I exclaimed. "And these others—they are Crusaders, too." One of the helmeted heads climbed up onto a battlement, to afford himself a better view of us. At the same time I heard a muted sound, the noise of a mechanism being cranked by hand, slowly but with a certain urgency.

I knew this sound well, and so did my companions. It was a crossbow being cocked.

"Don't cease talking," murmured Sir Nigel. "Soothing speech calms horses, hounds, and nervous sentries."

I said that we were honored to stand before this great city, and looked forward to seeing its many holy sites. I had the impression this guard knew exactly what I was saying—perhaps all visitors before the gates delivered similar sentiments. The speech he offered in return struck me at first as little more than polite-sounding noise. As he continued, however, I recognized that the language was enough like Latin for me to glean some meaning.

He believed us, he said, when we said that we were Crusaders. He was honored to see such noble *cavalieri. "Inglese?"* he inquired at last.

"Yes, every one of us," I said.

He reached down and produced the crossbow, painted blue and red along its stock, and decorated with yellow stars. A quarrel—a crossbow bolt—was ready-cocked. I had no doubt that a quarrel fired at such close range would pass right through me, and end up buried in the ground.

Edmund stepped before me, and said, looking upward, "No quarrel has the force to go through two men."

"*Corragio,*" said the bowman with a laugh.

A carter approached the gate from the road behind us with a load of charcoal. He called up to the battlement, but the guard explained that no one could pass for the moment. The sight of a guard leveling a crossbow caused no evident concern or surprise. Several other tradesmen arrived with heavily laden cobs, stout-legged horses. We all had to wait.

The barrier opened at last, nearly silent on its massive hinges.

A figure before us gave a bow—a young man with a striped tunic with a gold-colored belt. Every trade had its livery: the baker his cap, the brewer his long leather apron. I took this man to be a herald. He wore a finely wrought gipser purse and a silver-chased sheathe with a well-wrought hilt, and introduced himself as Fulke Mowbray, herald to King Richard's envoy in Rome. He gracefully motioned us inside the gate.

"Stay close to me," said the herald. "The Holy City is ripe with cutthroats."

TWENTY·FIVE

Just inside the city walls was a great church, and a vine-yard. A few rows of pear trees offered shade from the afternoon sun. I was not surprised that church clerks would want grapes for wine, or pears for perry, a pleasing drink.

But I was surprised at the shabbiness of the city, weeds and broken stones everywhere. We marched through flocks of sheep driven by shepherds armed with short swords and cudgels. Geese flocked along the broad, paved street.

Nevertheless, it was the grandest city I had ever seen. Father Giles had drawn sketches on my *tabela,* and described to me the magnificence of the Colosseum. But nothing prepared me for the sight of it, ghost-gray and gigantic. Edmund and I exchanged glances of wonderment and delight. The arches and barrel vaults that supported the great monument thrilled me. By comparison, the grandest church in Nottingham, and the richest oak-timbered hall of my father or his fellow merchants, were like the playhouses of little boys.

Sir Nigel, too, was flushed with excitement as we passed through the vast late-afternoon shadow of this place. And yet I continued to be surprised at how worn this holy site was. Much of the marble facing of the monuments had been stripped away, leaving holes where it had been attached. Men and women in rags crouched in the entranceways and corridors, and as they caught my glance they called out in tones of no great respect.

I was stunned further at the ruin of what I took to be the great Roman Forum, a place Father Giles had described to my family, my sister and both my parents all as rapt as I was to hear of this crossroads of an empire. Either a brutal army had swept through this civic core, or the rubble was all so much older than I could imagine. Oxen lowed in a make-shift pen, among fallen columns. Men in coarse-spun aprons fed lengths of marble into a kiln.

"They are turning chunks of pagan temples into lime, for stone mortar," explained Sir Nigel.

"Is it wise," I found myself asking, "to consume the famous ruins?"

"I think God takes no great offense," replied Sir Nigel.

Men in livery—fine, flowing silks—eyed us as we passed, swords cocked jauntily at their hips. They put their heads together and laughed, and I knew how shabby we looked, like prisoners or mendicant paupers, not at all like men-at-arms. And women would not give us a second glance—

well-formed, graceful women, enjoying the music of the fountains as they talked, ignoring us.

I hated our worn shoes, our monk-woven garments. I wanted to sing out that we were Crusaders, but I knew my carefully tutored Latin would sound stiff. Merchants and tradesmen took a moment to eye us. They were clad in bright clothing, the finest examples of the dyer's art. They turned back to their fruit stalls or their gossip, speaking a fluid, rapid tongue.

Our guards were heavy men, too fat for active battle, or thin and wide-eyed, youths pressed into service. At the corner of a narrow street the herald knocked at a studded oak door. A servant opened it and bowed courteously.

We were left alone in an outer chamber. Sir Nigel and Sir Rannulf consulted each other. An army of masons, they agreed, could not construct such a town, the existence of which, Sir Nigel asserted, was itself testimony to the glory of Our Lord.

Edmund and I stood shoulder to shoulder. This Holy City was a cold place, I thought, and I shivered.

We were taken into a room lit by tapers, fine candles, long and slender, that did not smoke and sputter as they burned.

There stood a man in a richly dyed scarlet mantle. The dancing candle shadows half hid him, but I could make out a short sword, with a red jasper decorating its hilt. He had fair eyebrows, nearly white eyelashes, and the thick muscular neck of a fighting man. Fulke the herald watched from the shadows.

The nobleman introduced himself as Luke de Warrene, a knight of the royal household, and steward to King

Richard's ambassador to Rome. He spoke in clear London English.

I gave the most flowery introduction I could manage, announcing the worshipful Crusaders Sir Nigel of Nottingham and Sir Rannulf of Josselin, and the squire-at-arms Edward Strongarm. "I am Hubert de Bakewell," I concluded, conscious of my own name's lack of poetry.

Sir Luke considered our names silently for a moment, like a man afraid of ill tidings. "How can I believe, my good squire, that you have set foot in the Holy Land?"

"My lord," I protested, "we are men of honor."

"Travelers have told many tales in recent weeks," said Sir Luke. "Or perhaps they aren't mere rumors. We hear that King Richard is imprisoned in Sicily, that he took a quarrel in the neck outside Acre, that he is buried on the shore there. How can I believe that you four know anything of Crusading?"

I could not hide my anger, but Sir Nigel gave my arm a squeeze. "You're doing surpassingly well, Hubert," he whispered.

Perhaps this emboldened me. I said, "And how can we trust you, my lord, to deserve an account of our travels?"

Sir Nigel hissed through his teeth.

"If you will," I was quick to add, "permit me to ask."

The mantle-clad man approached me.

He wore a brooch, and at the sight of it I was plunged into silence.

It was an enamel insignia, a leopard with his right paw upraised. While some called Richard *Lionheart,* and many praised the king's lionlike bravery, the royal symbol for his court was this leopard, an animal few Englishmen had ever seen in real life. It was a special kind of fighting cat, we believed, one especially noted for its courage.

The knight took my sword hand in his own, and examined the calluses along my palm, and the still-healing chafing on my forearm, the result of wearing chain mail in hot weather.

I continued to feel ashamed of my impertinence. I dropped to one knee, and when he bid me rise I obeyed, and said, "My lord, we have news of King Richard."

Again I wished I wore a sword. Sir Luke's mantle had been dyed with kermit-seed vermilion, the most expensive dye known.

"Acre has fallen," I said.

"The siege is broken?" he asked wonderingly.

"And the inhabitants put to the sword," I said.

He put his hands together prayerfully.

Then he said, "I have another question." His eyes said, *One I am afraid to put into words.*

"My lord, we remain at the service of the king," I said in my best court manner.

The nobleman stepped close to me, smelling of cloves, a rich spice dukes and other wealthy people chew to sweeten their breath. He said, nearly whispering, "Speak softly. There are spies, even here. Show no sign of your tidings in your eyes."

I nodded, indicating that I understood.

"Answer me," he said. "Is King Richard still living?"

Luke led us down corridors dimly illuminated by the late-day sun, past tall oak doors shut tight. I lingered behind, pleased to be in such a splendid house, polished stone tiles on the floors. I heard a whisper and stayed behind, gazing down a shadowy hallway.

A young woman gazed right back at me from a short distance away. She wore a gown with scarlet sleeves, a linen wimple around her throat. A lady-in-waiting stood just behind her, and I heard her offer the young woman an explanation of my presence: "A young knight, perchance, my lady."

The young woman gave me an appraising glance. She had green eyes, and held her hands clasped before her in the way ladies were trained. For some reason I was slow in remembering my lessons in courtesy. I gave a bow at last, but by then Nigel was calling, with what I thought was energetic coarseness, "Hubert, come see where you'll be sleeping off your travels."

Sir Luke read the look in my eyes as I hurried to join them.

"Perhaps you have seen Galena," he said. "Sir Maurice's daughter. She takes the air this time each day."

TWENTY·SIX

I never missed my family more than on that first misty morning in Rome, as Edmund and I walked out to the river, drinking in the vision of red roofs and spires.

My sister Mary and I used to build castles out of rough-hewn blocks, and put a flag at the peak of each rude tower, a tuft of my father's best wool felt. Now I heard bells from a dozen holy places. I was swept with emotion. I included my family in my prayers, and asked Heaven to keep them each out of harm's grasp.

"Here we see the Circus Maximus," said Fulke de Mowbray later that day. "A large empty field now, but you see the outline of the arena, where chariots raced. All adorned with rich jewels and golden helmets, the emperors would sit here and watch the contest."

"No one wears a helmet made of gold," said Edmund.

"These were emperors of an empire that stretched from Carthage to Persia," said Fulke. "Strong men. Gold helmets."

"Gold is both too heavy and too soft," said Edmund, lowering his head politely. "No doubt their helmets were tin, plated with the precious metal."

Fulke had been ordered by Sir Luke to take the two of us on a tour of the legendary sites, while Sir Luke attended the two knights on a similar series of visits. Fulke had made no attempt to disguise his boredom. As he recounted the storied wonders of Rome, his tone of impatience with two simple squires, still dressed in pilgrim's weeds while the tailors stitched our new clothes, was quite evident.

"And you, Hubert, doubted that a dragon sleeps under the temple of Vesta," said Fulke accusingly. He wore one blue stocking, one yellow. His belt had a silver buckle, and his sheathe had been polished overnight.

"It is possible," I said placatingly. "Perhaps. A dragon may sleep there—"

"Frozen to stone by a saint's curse," asserted Fulke.

"It may be so," I said.

"I tell you the great wizard Virgil carved the mask of Truth," said Fulke. "He did it so any liar putting his finger in the gaping mouth would have it bitten off—and you choose to not believe me."

"Virgil was a poet," I murmured, "not a wizard."

"I show you where hell opened up on Palatine Hill, and you say it is but a fine big hole in the ground."

My father had always said that legends are like flies, easy to breed and hard to swat dead. "I want to see real relics," I said earnestly. "The skull of Saint Agnes, the grave of Saint Peter. Take us to where holy martyrs burned to death to the glory of Heaven."

"Why did you leave King Richard's army?" asked Fulke.

"Sir Nigel was badly hurt—" I began.

"He looks sturdy enough," said Fulke.

"Heaven be thanked," said Edmund.

"You speak of Heaven, squire," said Fulke.

"That offends you?" I could not keep from asking.

Fulke had sturdy legs, a fact that his stockings were no doubt intended to display. If he knew how to flourish a blade, I believed, he could draw blood in a fight.

"You two footlings dare to utter the holy name of Heaven," Fulke said. "You who were not fit enough to win Jerusalem."

He turned and left us.

We were silent for a while.

It was a sunny noon. A beggar approached us, limping across the dried sheep dung and yellow grass of the Circus Maximus. Edmund gave him an entire round bread, a simnel loaf he had been saving for his midday meal.

"Do you think we can find Saint Peter's church by ourselves," said Edmund, "or do you think some gang of heralds will attack us?"

I said, "I think the danger is very great," just able to keep from laughing.

I went alone to the roof of the great house late that day. There among the pots of luxuriant rosemary and the late-season, white blossoms of the rose, I was not surprised to see Galena and her serving woman.

I made a better effort of introducing myself now, and she smiled knowingly, as though the house had been abuzz with news about the Crusading visitors. "I am pleased to know you, good Hubert," she said. "My father has needed some fighting men—Rome is not safe. And as for me—"

Here she stammered, and perhaps there was the slightest shyness about her manner. She wore a gown of *watchet,* a light blue fabric, and she wore her long brown hair in a plait down her back. I was garbed in a rude traveler's tunic—the tailor was outfitting Edmund in royal livery even now, and mine would be ready before we dined. I had brushed my simple garments before climbing the stairs to the roof, however, and had been careful to comb my hair.

She continued, after a long pause, "I am pleased to welcome you for my own sake."

"You can help protect my lady, when she visits her aunt," said the servant. "If it please you."

It was normal for servants to affect a loftier tone of conversation and dress than their charges. This attendant wore blue-dyed silk sleeves, and a coif of dazzling white linen.

"Quiet yourself, Blanche," said Galena. And to me she continued, "My aunt Alice is ill, in the convent of Saint Agnes, not far beyond the city walls. But with the streets so crowded with outlaws, I have been unable to visit."

"Are the street churls really so threatening?" I asked.

"Coarse creatures, and they barely deserve to be called men," sniffed Blanche, in excellent court Frankish.

"They are noble youths," said Galena, in English, "skilled at both broad and short swords. They have a great deal of time to plan mischief. They take hostages as a violent sport, and wait for payments of ransom. They have pikemen at their command, and they are indeed very dangerous."

She added, "Not, of course, for a Crusader."

TWENTY·SEVEN

"I am grateful to the saints for healing Sir Nigel's broken bones," said Sir Maurice de Gray, King Richard's envoy to Rome.

"We survive to serve our lord king," said Nigel.

We dined on *haslet,* roast entrails of deer, a favorite of royal hunters, and suckling pig. Boiled lamb was presented on a platter, and servants served us several sorts of wine: blood-thick red wine, sweet white wine, and every other hue and flavor of the vine. Our tablecloth was linen, woven in a pattern of triangles, pleasing to the eye and to the touch. Sir Maurice had announced that he was giving us an English feast to make us feel at home in this foreign land.

I was sorry that the Lady Galena had not joined us, but it was the custom among knights for men and women to dine apart. When a house servant brought a new plate, a turtle pie or lamprey eel in syrup, he bent his knee until Sir Maurice had agreed to allow the presented dish onto the table. A platter of fish maws, a famous court delicacy, was held out for Sir Maurice's inspection. He sniffed, and gave an apologetic smile.

"It's late in the fishing season," he explained. "Only the old, canny fish have survived so long, and sometimes their flavor is not good."

"So it would be if someone decided to feast on me," said Sir Nigel. "Or on Sir Rannulf, by my faith."

Rannulf tried to smile, his scarred face folding into a caricature of mirth.

Sir Luke had provided us with swords and sheaths, belts and shields, and a cobbler promised us in fractured English that we would soon have new footwear fit for fighting knights. We each possessed surcoats of wool, emblazoned with the royal leopard, his paw raised and his teeth bared in the snarl peculiar to the legendary beast.

Edmund had accepted a two-handed sword with thanks, there being no fighting hammer. He had been silently exultant at donning the *heg wedes*—fine garments. Edmund knew as well as I did that we had arrived to a position filled with possibility. In a matter of an hour or two we had risen from bedraggled pilgrims to a group of royal men-at-arms.

Sir Maurice was a banneret, the highest station of knighthood, a man who had won the personal trust of the crown. He was portly, with the sanguine complexion of a man who enjoyed his drink. His right eye was blind, scarred by a sword stroke that cleft his eyebrow and his cheek as well. Such a wound usually marks the end of a career—a man carrying a shield depends on his right eye. Nevertheless Sir Maurice had become an indispensable servant of the throne, and we were careful to speak our best Norman-Frankish.

"The farmland," said Sir Maurice, "is riddled with gangs of *brigantes,* rough youths untrained in war who play at being Crusaders. The real war goes on without them, so they harass the traveler." His remaining eye was green, like his daughter's, and he fixed us with it as though he could know what we thought as well as what we said.

I saw in Sir Maurice the sort of knight I wanted to be someday, and I wondered if Sir Nigel recognized in this dignified man the pinnacle of an ambition he might yet dream of fulfilling.

"The four of us fear no countryside, my lord," said Sir Nigel.

"If King Richard is killed on Crusade," Maurice continued, "the entire royal household, in London and abroad—chamberlains, ambassadors, down to the brewers and the bakers—are all released. The new king chooses his own castle keepers. And a new Roman envoy. You are Rome's first travelers from the Crusade, and you have seen the king alive."

"Alive among the enemy dead, Sir Maurice," said Sir Nigel.

"Have we sent many Infidels to hell?" asked Sir Maurice, in the tone of a man interrupting himself to make a polite inquiry.

"Many score of the enemy, my lord," said Sir Rannulf.

"Before King Richard departed on this holy Crusade," said Sir Maurice, "he made his brother Prince John swear not to set foot on English soil."

Sir Nigel set down his wine cup.

"Rumor is that Prince John readies a fleet to carry him to England. There he will do mischief." Sir Maurice poured wine for Sir Nigel, and for himself, and passed the pitcher down to us, a silver vessel with a gillyflower design all around. "I shall send Sir Luke to discover whether Prince John is in England, and to contrive to prevent him from doing harm if he is. Sir Luke will need armed companions. You will all leave for England as soon as the sea weather is safe."

I met Edmund's eye. I had described Lady Galena to my friend, and he had agreed with me that we should lend the young woman all the help in our power. "I ask your leave, Sir Maurice," I said, "for one further duty we may perform here in Rome."

Perhaps I surprised Sir Nigel by speaking up just then. It was something close to bad manners to address my superiors without their assent in such a circumstance, but once I had begun, I could not keep silent. "I ask permission for Edmund and myself to accompany the lady Galena on a visit to her ailing aunt."

Sir Maurice's reaction to this was a surprise to me. I expected eager gratitude and cheerful approval of this thoughtful request. Instead the old knight put a hand to his cheek, fingering the scar. "I was attacked thirty years ago—in Limoges by a drunken husband. I was not sober myself, and took a short sword to my face before I strangled him."

"With your naked hands?" asked Rannulf.

"One gloved, one bare," said Sir Maurice. "And you?" he asked pointedly, looking with grave curiosity at Rannulf.

The Crusader ran his tongue over his scarred lips. "I took a knife in my sleep at Caen. The squire of a knight I had unhorsed that day—a small, quick squire with hairy hands. He fed me a *dague,* a short knife, and nearly forced it down my throat." Rannulf flattened a crumb with his forefinger. "He escaped unhurt. Some nights I dream of cutting him into quarters."

I saw again Rannulf cutting the scavenger's throat just days before, and rising from the act with no apparent feeling.

"It's not the tournament that marks us," said Sir Maurice. "Or the war."

"Night fighting, cuckolds, and the rivals for women," said Rannulf. "They are more treacherous than the Infidel." He turned to Sir Nigel, adding, in a measured tone, "We should leave for England at once."

"The fighting in a city like this," agreed Sir Maurice, "can be deadlier than any joust. City felons have a special malice."

Nigel had been studying me. "My squire is as brave as any young man I have ever known. Both Hubert and Edmund have made worthy companions."

I cannot put into words the pride I felt then.

"You are blessed indeed," said Sir Maurice with a smile. "Such young men have a sterling future."

"Let the four of us," said Nigel, "accompany the lady Galena on this errand of charity."

Sir Maurice shook his head. "I fear you underestimate our Roman criminals."

"My lord," said Sir Nigel, "none of us has survived both Infidel and shipwreck by being foolish—or feeble."

Sir Maurice fixed me with his bright, green eye, and perhaps he could indeed see into my soul. He considered for a moment.

"Tomorrow you may accompany my daughter," he consented with a sigh. "My late wife's sister Alice Longfort suffers a palsy and is confined to the convent of Saint Agnes, outside the city walls."

Edmund leaned forward into the candlelight, looking every bit as pleased as I felt.

"Wear your swords," added the banneret. "And be prepared to use them."

TWENTY-EIGHT

"My family have been heralds," said Fulke Mowbray, "since the Battle of Hastings."

The morning was cloudless.

We wore light armor and our new royal surcoats, Fulke outdoing himself in finery, scarlet stitchery around the yellow royal leopard on his breast. The morning was so chilly our breath flickered white at our lips. Edmund and Rannulf stood at a slight distance from me outside the convent walls, Rannulf gesturing and parrying imaginary blows as he recounted some memorable feat of arms for Edmund's benefit. Nigel stood with folded arms, looking every bit the worldly Crusader, the sunlight in his silver hair. He smiled and nodded at the female servants on their way to market, and they whispered, eyeing us as they scurried past.

Galena and her servant Blanche de Lille were inside, behind stout wooden gates, visiting the ailing gentlewoman.

"We have suffered the arrogance," Fulke continued, "and, if you will forgive me, the ignorance of knights and squires all those years. We observe them trade insults and watch them puff up and try to kill each other with every clumsiness imaginable."

"There are prideful knights, it's true," I said, thinking of Sir Jean and his golden-haired squire, somewhere well on their way to England. It was also true that, despite the stories of brave battles, actual fighting was an ugly, wasteful business.

"A knight called Gregory le Goff," Fulke added, "struck my father some years ago—I can barely describe the act."

"It galls me to hear it," I said truthfully.

"He slapped my good, wise father with his bare hand, one midsummer night during the revels at Honfleur."

Midsummer nights were well known as occasions of drinking and fornication under the starry sky. Midsummer celebrations led to pregnancy and broken noses, as everyone knew. To be struck with a glove, or even a gloved hand, betokened a certain rough respect. A blow with a naked fist, while likely to be less injurious, was particularly insulting.

"Custom," said Fulke, "did not allow my father to challenge this drunken knight to a joust."

"But a herald is a man of good name," I protested. "A knight would have gladly defended your father's honor."

Fulke wore a pained expression. "My family is proud, and suffers insult in manly silence."

"If I had been there," I said, "I would have won an apology from this Gregory le Goff."

"Sir Gregory died a week before Michaelmas that year," said Fulke, "drowned in a puddle outside the north gate of Chester."

"Mourned only by his family, no doubt."

Fulke gave a slight bow. "If I had known you were willing to aid Lady Galena," he confided, "I would not have been so tart with you."

We had accompanied the Lady Galena and her attendant Blanche de Lille along a broad avenue, passing through the city gate, and traveling the Via Nomentana to a handsome church and convent. We had passed fruit stalls and stonecutters, monks sweeping the byways, and children tossing balls of wax and twine, but nowhere had we seen any evidence of armed men.

But there had been watchers—silent, robed figures leaning in doorways, ducking back into shadows.

"There will be bloodshed today," said Fulke pensively. He wore an *anlass,* a short sword, at his hip, and had brought only a small target shield. Heralds dressed in the finest livery, but were not expected to go heavily armed.

In the many weeks before this, I had sometimes pretended a courage I did not feel. When I recalled the carnage of Acre—and I worked hard to force the images from my mind—I could not imagine putting myself or my companions through a similar experience. At that moment, however, I was genuinely indifferent to whether fighting came my way. I was even hopeful that some noble *bravi* might suffer punishment at my hand—if it served Galena's interest.

Fulke might have sensed my willingness to do battle, because he added, "Beware of a man wearing yellow silk."

I had to laugh at this ominous-sounding advice. "Did you seek the help of a ghost-wife, Fulke?"

Ghost-wives were legendary fortune-tellers, able to raise phantoms and deliver the most telling omens.

Fulke gave a smile. "His name is Tomasso Orsino, and he studied sword fighting with Sir Baldwin of Bec."

Baldwin of Bec was a legendary knight, by reputation the killer of scores of men. There were many songs about his prowess, and about his death a few years before, falling from a tower in Constantinople.

"Tomasso has a small army of pikemen," Fulke further advised. "And he would love nothing better than to steal Lady Galena right out of our hands."

Lady Galena and Blanche joined us outside the convent walls, thanking us graciously for allowing this visit, and reporting that Lady Alice had been well enough to share a dish of stewed figs.

"They were flavored with cinnamon," said Blanche, eager to show her appreciation for expensive pleasures.

"But we would have savored stony bread," said Galena, "just as happily for the opportunity to see my dear aunt, and I thank you, every one, again for this blessing." She had, I do believe, an especially meaningful glance for me as she said this.

We rode back to the Porta Pia, and passed through the impressive city gate. Edmund and Rannulf went on before us, bareheaded but carrying their bucklers. Fulke and I followed. All of us, including the ladies, were mounted on gentle, soft-mouthed palfreys, the sweetest-tempered sort of steed, nearly every breed of warhorse having been taken by the Crusade.

Nigel brought up the rear—he and Rannulf had noted more than once that the rear guard should always be an experienced swordsman.

We made our way into a side street, our passage blocked by an overturned cart and a scattering of sacks of meal. I thought nothing of this accident, or of the two carters going about the business of stacking the spilled sacks. But as we detoured into a narrow street, with overhanging balconies and deep shadows, despite the late morning, I puzzled over the furtive slowness with which the carters had gone about their duty.

I knew for certain that something was wrong when I heard the long, chiming hiss of Edmund drawing his two-handed blade, and the *chik-chik* of Rannulf urging his palfrey forward, the mount snorting, frightened.

Someone gave a shout, and the portals up and down the street opened.

Out poured armed men.

TWENTY·NINE

Many warhorses love the sound of battle and prick up their ears with excited pleasure at the clash of steel on shield.

Our city horses, soft-mouthed and unused to clamor, panicked.

I found no way to strike an accurate blow with my sword, even as several eager hands tugged at me, pulling on my mail skirt, seizing my leg. Galena called out, and to my surprise and relief she produced a knife from within her cloak, and slashed about her at the hands that tried to drag her from the saddle. Our attackers were outfitted with cudgels, staffs, and short swords, and some fought with one hand while flourishing a wineskin in the other. There was a howl as she sliced a hairy wrist, and another just as anguished as she cut open a wine sack, held up as an improvised buffer against her dagger.

Without warning I was unseated and sprawling in the muddy gutter down in the middle of the street. It was one of the primary rules of war—a mounted man has power over footmen, both psychological and tactical. Now I had lost that advantage, although I was quick in regaining my feet.

The closeness of my immediate assailant's body kept my weapon angled downward, so I struck him on the bridge of his nose with the edge of my buckler. He cut at the air with his short sword, baring his teeth, and I sliced his neck with my blade. Drawing back a half step, and taking a stance, I readied a fatal stroke, commending my adversary's soul to Heaven.

He dodged my death cut, my sword striking sparks from the stone wall. He lunged low, his blade driving toward my privy parts, his sword wounds sucking and rasping. He darted and feinted, fighting with a bloody grimace. But I was fast, and my attack was steady. My teachers would have been proud as my opponent weakened, stanching the wound in his neck with one hand, making erratic swipes with the other. He faded, fled, and I took a moment to consider our position.

Galena was safe, still mounted, the knife in her hand. Fulke was wrestling with a wiry little man, and our herald looked equal to the challenge. Edmund chopped at his opponents with the determination of a woodsman. Edge blows are all that matter with a big sword, and the two-handed broadsword was smithed and honed with a large man like Edmund in mind. My friend's lack of experience kept him flat-footed, but his heavy sword knocked his assailant down with a sickening, snapping sound from somewhere in the attacker's body, a rib or shoulder breaking.

Rannulf was punishing a knot of assailants, and I could tell by Nigel's snarling, "Drop your swords, by Jesu," that he needed little help. I seized the bridle of Galena's horse but was too out of breath to utter any reassurance. Blanche was white-faced, clinging to the neck of her mount, but Galena's voice was steady when she said, "Are you hurt, good Hubert?"

Someone lifted a command, and our attackers fled, a clumsy, wine-soaked retreat. Footsteps splashed the gutter, and wounded men were hauled along and into the waiting doorways. The street was silent except for the shuddering of our mounts and the clapping, aimless flight of pigeons far above.

"Are you hurt?" she asked again.

I told her I was uninjured, and asked, with what I realized was, under the circumstances, a nearly comical courtliness, "And do I see you well?"

"Quite well, good Hubert, and thank you."

"You may sheathe your blade, my lady," I said with a breathy laugh.

She slipped the dagger back into her cloak with a practiced air. Fulke was breathing heavily but uninjured, slumped against the wall. Edmund was freckled with gore and panting hard; he reported that he was not wounded, either. His voice was high-pitched with relief. "All well, Hubert. All sound and well."

Rannulf had found a long, thin knife with an extravagant amber hilt, dropped by one of our attackers. He was examining it in a lance of sunlight, when he looked up and said, "Listen!"

Liste!

THIRTY

A tangle of footmen, their halberds clattering together, advanced on us from the street ahead.

Behind them on a well-muscled steed rode a man with a yellow tunic and a flowing yellow cap. Drawing a broadsword with a flourish, he gave a piercing whistle that echoed in the narrow street. The remaining mob of assailants limped from doorways and did what they could in our rear, harassing Sir Nigel.

I've always particularly hated the halberd. Edmund and I had agreed that our great fear is that one of these cruel, long-shafted weapons might gouge out our eyes—or some other essential organ. Rannulf started in on the attackers, quick with his sword, and the weapons were proving clumsy, the shafts too long for this crowded little street. The pikemen themselves were knock-kneed and unsteady, wine spilling from their goatskin sacks.

Throwing my buckler to one side, I seized Galena's palfrey by the reins, and leaped into the saddle of my own wild-eyed mount. Nigel was fighting effectively, laying about him with his sword, but unable to be of any further help to us as we rode past him. A blade ripped the hem of my surcoat, and another barked the leather of my gauntlet. I kicked one attacker in the mouth, more or less accurately, and urged my mount forward, pulling Galena's horse along.

I kept one hand tight around Galena's reins, until we were all the way across a large, sunlit square. Blanche followed on her mount—hunched, a hood over her head. Galena was laughing. "How far do we have to ride, Hubert," she called, "before we are safe?"

"No distance is too far," I said, "if it pleases you."

"Are all squires," she asked, "so well spoken?"

I gave her a wordless smile, shaking so much inwardly that I could make little in the way of further conversation.

The two carters with their scattered sacks of meal had righted the wagon, a pair of oxen lowing with a dull, heartfelt impatience. The two wagon drivers now took a moment to listen to the clash and outcry of fighting that echoed from the narrow street. They put their heads together, a sluggish caricature of conspiracy. Then one of them drew a weapon from within the bags of flour, a rusty broadsword.

I thanked Heaven that these two men were as drunk as all our other attackers this fine noon. My complaining palfrey tossed and snorted, foam flying, but I beat the carters with the flat of my sword, and sent the two of them flying.

Sir Maurice met us outside the iron-studded door of his house, splendid in freshly oiled mail.

Tomasso Orsino, without his yellow cap, his silk tunic torn and soaked with blood—not, it seemed, his own—sat on a weary palfrey. Sir Rannulf rode beside him, so close that the two appeared to be companions, except that Tomasso's sheath carried no weapon.

The Roman nobleman was pleasant looking, with a small, pointed beard. He was more than a few years older than Edmund and I, with the deep chest and thick neck of a man who both ate well and practiced swordplay. Sir Nigel walked behind him, bereft of his buckler but apparently unhurt. Fulke and Blanche brought up the rear, looking exultant.

Sir Maurice had evidently received word of our trouble, and had been on the verge of leaving to join us. The banneret wore a sword with a golden pommel, a dagger in a sheath on the other hip.

"Are you harmed?" he asked his daughter sharply.

"Father, I am not," she said.

"In any way?" he asked.

"No, please Heaven," she responded.

He breathed a prayer.

Then, pointedly ignoring our prisoner, like a man in the most ordinary circumstance, he went on to ask his daughter, "And how was the health of the noble lady, your aunt?"

"Worshipful and sound," she replied, "in flesh and soul."

"It pleasures me to hear it," said Sir Maurice, and then, as though just now recognizing a guest, he smiled and exclaimed something in the Roman tongue.

Tomasso replied with an equally studied air, artful and

convincing, words that conveyed the meaning, *I have come to visit you with my new English friends.*

The sound of approaching footsteps and the clang of steel against armor reached us from an adjoining street. Tomasso straightened in his saddle and smiled, and Nigel drew both his *couteau* and his broadsword; a knight who had lost his shield often defended himself with a weapon in each hand.

"That, my lords," said Fulke, with his lofty herald's accent, "will be a mob of Orsini cousins, ready to dispute Tomasso's capture."

Thirty-one

I sat beside a large red clay urn that was bursting with rosemary, the fragrant medicinal herb luxuriating in the afternoon sun.

I turned at the sound of a step nearby, but to my surprise it was Nigel. He was dressed in a smock of rich blue, a leopard in scarlet on his breast. Hours before, we had hurried through the gates of the envoy's dwelling, and Fulke had successfully persuaded the Orsini allies to retreat and be prepared to negotiate for Tomasso's release.

"I'm told," said my master, "that if I stand way over at one end of this roof garden, I can gaze across the River Tiber and see the tomb of Hadrian the Great."

I hid my disappointment that my visitor was not the person I had been expecting. "A great emperor of Rome," I said, remembering my studies. "He mastered the pagan tribes of England, or do I confuse him with some other champion?"

"He's long reduced to bone dust, I'm sure. But his monument remains."

I wondered if Nigel, who was capable of both interesting and tedious discourse, had climbed the stairs to provide me with a lesson in Roman history.

I had been wanting to ask all afternoon, "How did Sir Rannulf capture Tomasso?"

"In my friend's usual manner," said Nigel. "He took a blow or two, I'm sorry to say, but then he used his sword to snap a few halberds. He killed Tomasso's horse with one blow to the neck—you've seen it done—and then he stood, one foot on the stunned Roman's throat until the fellow had wits enough to surrender. I believe Rannulf would have killed him, if I hadn't asked him not to."

"It was not a pretty fight?"

"Is it ever?" Nigel laughed.

"What will Sir Maurice do with Tomasso?" I asked.

"Treat him well, with meat and drink," said Nigel. "Politics is often a matter of taking hostages, and holding them until some favor is produced. These Romans are accustomed to this—it is a dangerous sport, I believe. Sometimes the lord Pope helps negotiate a particularly difficult agreement."

"Perhaps," I said with a laugh, "I am fortunate to be so ignorant of the ways of great cities."

"I have tidings for you, Squire Hubert," said Sir Nigel, sitting down beside me. "Sir Maurice has offered you a position, here in Rome."

"Doing what duty, my lord?" I managed to stammer.

"The lady Galena, it seems, has high praise for your alertness and courage today. If you wish to be an assistant to the royal envoy in Rome, and learn the ways of royal intrigue, here is your future."

And, I told myself, if I wished to stay close to the envoy's daughter.

"And you, my lord—would you be able to stay?"

"I have a mission to London with Sir Luke." Neither Nigel nor Rannulf had admired King Richard's prowess as a commander. It was true, however, that Richard was an anointed monarch, and the opportunity to serve him was an honorable way to secure the future.

"And Edmund?"

"The position is yours alone, Hubert—if I give my consent. Edmund will travel with us to England, and we leave tomorrow on a trip that could take months."

A richly detailed vision rose within me—a dream of myself as an envoy in the making, ordering servants, receiving messengers, washing my hands in a wide, silver bowl held by a servant.

A dream of taking Galena in my arms.

Rome is a city of bells, every church and chapel sounding forth its glory. Now a distant bell beat out a cascade of sounds, and where a moment before I had heard only a bell's clapper striking bronze, now I heard the far-off bell make a sound like words: *Stay here, stay here.*

Or was it *Go home, go home*?

THIRTY-TWO

"Look!" exclaimed Maurice. "See here what the kitchen servants found in the gizzard of tonight's goose."

He held up a coin and passed it around, the inscription and profile on the money worn nearly smooth.

We were dining, as before, without Galena, although Tomasso joined us, dressed in a sunny tunic, an amber ring on his forefinger. Two spearmen accompanied us tonight, standing against the wall, and Rannulf kept a pleasant but proprietary eye on our prisoner-guest. Occasionally Tomasso ran his eyes over to the shadowy spearmen and back to Rannulf, who met the Roman's glance with a friendly glance of his own. The two made efforts to communicate, searching for common words for *salt, bread, bruise.*

Rannulf's brow was discolored, and a cut along his neck bore a smear of medicine, some knight's concoction no doubt, perhaps carrot root and cooking grease. Rannulf often behaved like a man who believed himself made of hardwood—but he was not.

I had not discussed the opportunity Sir Maurice had offered me with anyone—and certainly not with Edmund. I suffered keen inward turmoil, even the freshly baked bread tasteless in my mouth. I wished I could ask Father Giles for advice on how to guess the will of Heaven.

"I've seen objects show up in fowl from time to time, my lord," Nigel was saying. "I believe there are English geese that feed strictly on lost buttons."

"And I heard of a goose cut open in Derby," I said, "with a red agate ring in its crop."

Tomasso listened to our conversation, perhaps with a little comprehension, and passed the coin along to Edmund.

"But surely," said Sir Maurice, with a slightly exasperated smile, "it is just a little unusual to find gold in the innards of the evening's meal."

"It isn't fine gold, my lords," said Edmund. "If you'll permit me—it's copper with a bare alloy of gold and perhaps tin."

"Ah," said Sir Maurice. He took a sip of wine, and inquired, "And how does a squire from Nottingham know that?"

Edmund blushed, his eyes suddenly downcast. "No doubt I'm mistaken, my lord."

Sir Nigel held out his cup for more wine, and a servant filled it to the brim. "Since we are all men-at-arms together," said Nigel, "and we all count ourselves loyal, squire and knight, I may explain Edmund's expertise on the subject of debased coinage, with the permission of my lord."

Nigel gave a graceful, brisk account of Edmund's em-
ployer and master, the late moneyer Otto, who had been
killed by the Exchequer's men. Edmund himself had faced
brutal punishment, and Nigel recounted Edmund's appoint-
ment as his squire by the lord sheriff of Nottingham. Sir
Nigel offered, in conclusion, the opinion that Edmund had
"proved himself equal to any squire on Crusade."

"More than equal," said Rannulf.

"I was blessed in my master," said Edmund, with the
earnest directness that marked so much of his speech, "and
in my friend." With this last remark he gave me a warm
glance.

"Heaven's blessing on us all," said Sir Maurice, evidently
pleased. Every good-hearted Christian loves a story of a sinner earning God's forgiveness, especially on the field of
battle.

"Which man of us," Rannulf surprised me by saying,
"does not have sins that require cleansing with enemy
blood?"

"Which indeed?" said Sir Maurice. The banneret frowned
thoughtfully, and ran a finger over his lips. "But I hope you'll
not take offense if I have one suggestion for all of you."

"A suggestion from you, my lord," said Nigel, taking
another long drink of wine, "is worth more than any gizzard
trove."

"Be wary," said Sir Maurice, "of enemies on your return
to England."

"Who would challenge the four of us, my lord?" inquired
Nigel.

"None of us is safe," said Maurice.

149

"I pray God I have no enemies," said Edmund, sounding shaken.

"Of course you don't," responded Sir Maurice good-naturedly. "But I myself fear Prince John is stealing into power in London."

I felt a chill in my belly, spreading out into my limbs. "What can the prince do there, my lord?" I asked.

"Our own King Richard," Maurice continued, "God's chosen monarch, is afraid that his own brother might creep like a creature on many little legs onto the throne."

The banneret lowered his voice. "Edmund, if anyone spreads the slander that you did not acquit yourself bravely during battle, or that you continued the sin of thievery while you voyaged, then you will face punishment on your return—as though you had never joined these worthy knights on Crusade."

THIRTY-THREE

That night rain pattered on the shuttered window. I could not sleep.

I prayed to Saint Julian, the patron saint of wanderers in special need. I understood that only seamen and carters prayed to such a saint. My family kept faith a simple, correct matter, never dreaming of soiling our knees in sudden prayer, like the devout plowman frightened by thunder.

But lying there in my bed, I felt the tug of Heaven.

I had already made my decision, as soon as I heard Sir Maurice's warning.

Just before we left Nottingham—it seemed a lifetime ago—Nigel had received a warrant for Edmund's further arrest. Nigel had ignored the warrant with a dry laugh, explaining that it lacked an official seal. I wondered now whether people in positions of power might continue to consider Edmund a felon.

Especially if someone arrived there before us, to slander my friend.

I rose from my bed in the predawn gray and scurried through the house, hurrying from hall to corridor, until I could follow the sound of voices.

Sir Maurice and Sir Nigel were sharing their morning wine, dipping white bread into the beverage—the morning meal of noblemen.

"I shall give you a letter of credence," Sir Maurice was saying, indicating a sealed scroll at his elbow. "Unless you run afoul of Prince John's men, you shall pass every sentry without any trouble."

I knelt before them and waited for them to realize I was there.

"A squire joins us," said Nigel.

"Does he?" said Sir Maurice, and I realized, with some embarrassment, that I had been on his blind side.

"Good morning to you both, my lords," I said, still kneeling.

"Ah," said Sir Maurice, endowing the syllable with a dignified sorrow. "I can tell by the sword at your side what your decision turns out to be."

"Hubert, you understand that I could forbid you to depart with us," said Nigel. "I could choose to command you, on pain of punishment, to serve the worthy envoy here in Rome, whether you wish it or not."

"My lords," I began, Nigel's remark causing me pain. "I pray your forgiveness if I've offended."

"Rise up, good Squire Hubert," said Maurice with a laugh. "And save your strength for a long and bitter voyage to our unsettled home."

Edmund and I were in the cellar of the envoy's house, meeting with Anselm Waybridge, the armorer. Rannulf had directed us to this craftsman's attention, saying that our weapons would benefit from care before our travels.

The armorer used a *fylor,* a rasping metal tool, to put an edge on our swords. The armorer was English, attached to Sir Maurice's household, but came from a corner of the kingdom where some local dialect and a bristling accent made it very difficult for us to understand him. This occurrence was fairly common—one hundred miles from home the innkeepers spoke foreign-sounding words. But this man made every effort to speak as we did, even hazarding a little Frankish, and the result was a halting, confused—if friendly—conversation.

"No one wants to go on a journey," he seemed to say, "without a keen-edged sword."

"No, we certainly don't," I agreed.

He made a motion of waves with his hands, and indicated that the sea—perhaps he meant the salt air—was not good for sword metal.

Edmund and I agreed heartily.

Anselm peered along the edge of my weapon, where the blade had struck the wall. He offered something critical about my luck, or the hardness of the wall, but smiled and said that a few licks of his tool would set it right.

A step whispered, and I turned.

"If the good Squire Hubert," said Blanche in a stiff, haughty tone, "could spare only one moment of his very precious time."

Galena's usually plaited hair had been brushed over her shoulders. Her silk gown whispered when she moved. When she passed before the light that spilled through a window, the morning sun illuminated the sea-blue folds of her garment.

"I understand," she said, "that you have decided to leave for England today."

"I follow my duty," I said, hating the wooden sound of my own speech.

Women did not usually appear before men with their hair down, preferring to have it plaited, veiled, or fully covered. These long, loose tresses betokened illness, or even bereavement. Her hair caught the light as she paced, and she spoke as though to Blanche, barely looking at me.

"Duty," she said, "is evidently both a complicated and powerful force—little understood by women."

There is an art of conversation known to courtly folk. A man seeking to discuss carnal affection might touch upon the subject of the loom, the bobbing of the loom weight, the passing in and out of scarlet thread among the beige. I had heard enough poetry to attempt such conversation—when my wits were not clouded by feeling.

But now my mouth spoke words without my ability to

choose or to stop them. "I will dream of this city," I said. "And of you."

I had never made such a bold—and truthful—assertion to a woman in my life.

Galena stopped pacing and looked at me. "I wish it were so," she said.

"My lady, I will come back to Rome," I said. "If it is in my power."

Blanche stopped me on the stairs, just before the cellar door. "My lady means to extend her wishes for a safe journey," she said, slightly out of breath.

Heavyhearted, it was all I could do to murmur thanks.

"And she wishes you might remember her, good Hubert, if I may say so on her behalf." I was surprised at the sudden sincerity in this proud servant's voice. "She offers you this locket, if it please you."

I closed my hand around a small object on a slender chain.

THIRTY·FOUR

I did not see Galena when we left the envoy's house, although I looked back several times to gaze up at the many shuttered windows.

When we reached the gates of Rome and bid farewell, Fulke took off his cap and gave a bow to each of us as we passed. I brought up the rear, and my horse nearly took fright at the all-but-silent creak of the city gate. The nervous gelding pissed a great gush and trembled, wild-eyed, at the sight of a gate man smiling and scratching his face.

Fulke made a flourish with his cap and an elaborate bow. His lips were scabbed from the street fight, and one eye was swollen.

"God be with you, herald," I said, keeping my voice steady.

"Sit your horse squarely, if you can, squire," said Fulke, offering a touch of friendly insult to take the edge off my sorrow—and, perhaps, his.

As we rode, I examined the *tressour* I had received from Blanche, a silver-framed locket holding a honey-bright slip of hair.

Edmund studied it respectfully, and gave it back. "You won her favor," he said simply.

"Perhaps she gives out bits of her hair broadcast, like a sower spreading seed." I did not mean this at all, but was trying to spare my friend's feelings. I marveled at my own good fortune. Certainly Edmund was tall enough and well favored enough to have won Galena's attention.

He smiled. "I don't think she does."

At first I paid no heed to the hunting party as it approached.

Sir Luke put a hand on his sword and turned in his saddle. "Those are the Orsini and the Neri," he said. "And other cousins and friends of our guest Tomasso."

The hunting party grew closer, with gleaming spurs, the hooded falcons cocking their blind heads, listening. The brush beaters flicked the air with their leather flails, and a few hares dangled from a huntsman's knot, bloodied where the falcons had seized them. Other coneys had been shot down by an archer, scored through with holes. The hunters

157

looked much like English barons out on a fine day, and yet the sheen of their horses, the cut of the plumes in the caps, all looked both foreign and handsome.

Sir Luke was garbed in an indigo-blue mantle, with brass-studded leather shoes, a man of wealth dressed simply for a journey. The rest of us were unmistakably King Richard's men, down to the leopard insignia on our breasts. None of us carried lances, but we all wore broadswords. There were six of us—Sir Luke had joined our usual foursome, and an ostler attended us, to take the horses back to Rome when we had embarked.

"Proud-looking men, aren't they?" said Nigel. There were a dozen of them, not counting the beaters.

"There's only one archer," said Rannulf. "He must be very skilled."

Many of the hunters wore swords, too, heavily armed for a day running down rabbits. No doubt they had decided to try for a variety of quarries—hope for Englishmen, but settle for field hares if necessary. The archer, a slim, clean-shaven man, slipped an iron-tipped arrow from his quiver, testing the point with his thumb.

The bowman made a fine sport of discussing with his companions which of us he would unhorse first, nodding and chuckling.

Rannulf turned off the road and rose challengingly in his saddle. Edmund joined him—a squire always shadowed his master. I could tell by the defensive set of my friend's shoulders that he did not like the odds.

One of the hunters called out words I could make out

only after a moment. *"La donna Galena,"* he cried mockingly, making rude, rutting gestures with his fist.

I kicked my mount and would have bounded across the field toward these laughing hunters—but Nigel seized my bridle.

THIRTY-FIVE

The hunters mocked us, jeered, and made every variety of coarse gesture, but Nigel restored me to reason by his cheerful example, he and Rannulf guarding our retreat all the way to the shore.

We boarded a weather-blackened cog, a stout, single-masted ship. The vessel smelled of manure and hay, but all the horses had disembarked weeks ago, in the Holy Land. The sailors were busy scrubbing the last traces of horse from the hold, and a carpet was put down in a cabin for Sir Luke, one of the wine-red tapestries taken in battle from the Saracens.

The *Saint Susanna* was loaded now with drink, newly built casks seeping black wine. Sir Nigel said, with a laugh, that he might be able to ride out another storm if he turned his belly into a wineskin. Sir Rannulf strode about the deck, as though eyeing the various vantage points from which he would kill boarders. The ship was outfitted with oriflammes—long, tapered banners that danced and fluttered in the wind. And to my surprise and pleasure, our ship also flew a leopard banner, a blue field displaying the warlike cat.

When the vessel was under sail, knifing through the rising mountains of water, Edmund and I climbed like veterans up and down the deck, trying to reassure ourselves that this ship was safe, that our return home was blessed, that it was only a matter of time before we set foot in the kingdom of our birth.

We had as much red Lombard wine as we could drink, and when the ship stopped to take on a fresh supply of ducks and suckling pigs, we dined as well as any lord. We supped each night with the captain, an Englishman from Whitby. John Hawkmoor knew the stories of the virgin martyrs by heart, and told us these tales during the long, cold evenings. Even Sir Rannulf took an interest in these legends of piteous martyrs.

Throughout the winter there were days when the ship made no headway, the small rain drifting down.

Sir Nigel began to bleed from his gums, and some nights he drank as much as he could hold, and more, until he spewed red wine and I had to help him to his berth. Sir Rannulf had sores on his lips, and paced the deck with a mood caused by what a surgeon would have recognized as *melas-khole,* an excess of black bile.

Edmund and I kept our spirits, practicing sword work on sunny afternoons, one hand clinging to rigging to help our balance, pretending to be mortally wounded, falling, rising, time and again. Laughing, forgetting all the real agony we had seen.

I believed that we were approaching safety, all danger done. Soon I would see my parents and my sister Mary, and wake to hear the familiar street songs of home.

Later I would marvel at my folly.

THIRTY-SIX

I had seen a winking point of light in the darkness, but now that I had my friend's attention, the light was gone.

"I don't see anything," said Edmund, "but mouse-gray water and rat-gray sky."

Edmund and I had speculated that we were close to our homeland, but the last approach to the shore was reputed to be the most frustrating part of any voyage, the winds contrary and the seas rough. The sailors had ceased to estimate our position on the coast, but their manner was quicker than ever, their eyes alight.

It was about the hour of sunset, although the actual *sol* himself had been a well-guarded secret, somewhere beyond the overcast for days.

"There it is!" I cried.

I had seen this furtive point of light fixed along the horizon—not bobbing or moving along like one of the shore craft we had seen all winter. Steady—not like a watchman's beacon, wavering with his steps.

Each sailor shook his head, or offered mysterious counsel: "Best wait and see, my lords," or "I don't think I see it, Squire Hubert."

I knew why.

They were wisely afraid that now we had come this far, some great menace would lift up out of the waves. And drown us all.

Sir Nigel said it could be a candle set on some old shipwreck, to keep sailors from running into it. Sir Rannulf, preferring a violent view of events, said a vessel must have caught fire.

Edmund asked our captain when he appeared, stiff-legged with the cold.

"It's the Southampton Lamp," said Captain Hawkmoor without looking to see for himself.

We were unwilling to ask further, too excited.

The captain leaned forward, as though confiding a secret in his flat, unemotional way. "The lamp is a big lantern." *A bigge lanthorn.* "Set out each night to mark the harbor."

We were afraid to look at each other.

"God help you, squires," said John. "It's England!"

THIRTY·SEVEN

We sailed up the brown river toward London the next afternoon, aided by the incoming tide.

Edmund and I waved at field men carrying wooden shovels and shepherd's crooks in the early spring afternoon. The men waved back, and children scurried along the riverbank, calling just as children everywhere at the passing of a ship. When I lifted my hand to salute a boy, he took a long moment before lifting his arm in return, and I wondered how we must all look to the very young.

"I see a tree full of rooks!" cried Edmund.

I saw it too, a great leafless oak crowded with a hundred black, squabbling, laughing birds. In no other land had I seen any fowl so eager to congregate as our common farmland rooks. The scent of mud and livestock, pigs and cattle, lightened our hearts. Sir Nigel clung to the salt-stiffened rigging to see out beyond the sedge and reeds.

"I spy Englishwomen!" said Sir Nigel. Goose girls in white aprons, dairywomen chasing hens with butter paddles. I wondered what Galena was doing just then—perhaps listening to some new, golden-voiced traveler, being won over by his charms.

When the wind was not sufficient, the captain ordered out two great sweeps, long spruce-wood oars, that sailors manned, two to an oar. The *Saint Susanna* proceeded up the river, and river men sculling along made way for us with open smiles, pleased, I thought, to see the faded leopard banner at our mast.

In late afternoon three horsemen in black leather rode beside the river, less than a stone's throw away.

"What ship is that?" called the lead man, every bit of metal he wore, from spurs to finger rings, shining. Customs officials always queried a ship from foreign parts, and these men looked like Exchequer's men, required to collect port fees and taxes.

John Hawkmoor identified our ship, and added, "She carries Lombard wine and a dispatch from the royal envoy in Rome."

The three duty collectors put their heads together, and the lead man called out, "What men are you?"

Sir Nigel had been listening to this with an easy smile, but now he turned to Sir Rannulf and muttered something in a low voice.

John Hawkmoor called out, identifying Sir Luke, Sir Nigel, and Sir Rannulf. "And two squires, with a shipload of able men, by Our Lady's grace."

"What squires have you?" asked the leather-voiced horseman.

Sir Nigel put a hand on John's sleeve. Sir Nigel himself called out, "The Crusading squires Hubert of Bakewell and Edmund Strongarm."

The three men consulted, then they turned their pale, clean faces toward us. As carefully as we had shaved, peering into our polished metal mirrors, and as thoroughly as we had washed our fustian blouses and our wool mantels, I realized we looked travel-stained and shabby compared with these city men.

When the horsemen observed Edmund standing in the stern, the lead man pointed, nodding, commenting to his companions. My friend had thrown a hood over his head at the sound of his name and bent over slightly, a big man trying to grow small.

The lead man's question rang out, "Is Edmund of Nottingham the moneyer's apprentice among you?"

Sir Nigel hissed, "Say nothing, any of you."

Sir Luke was the only one of us who looked like he had just stepped from a castle keep, the salt flecks brushed from his long blue cloak. He climbed so high on the freeboard rail that Sir Nigel seized his sleeve to keep him from toppling.

He sang out, "God keep King Richard!"

"King Richard and Prince John!" came the response from the riverbank.

Th,irty-eight

And Prince John.

"Not the very words," said Nigel, "that we wanted to hear."

"It will be dark by the time we dock in London," said John Hawkmoor, "with Our Lady's help."

"Darkness is no man's friend," said Sir Rannulf. "It helps us, and it helps them."

"But my lords," I could not keep myself from saying, "we're home, nearly, and our fighting is done."

Never had I felt less like helping Sir Nigel buckle on a sword. All the fighting I had seen, with lance and halberd, shield and dagger, seemed to me at that moment worse than pointless. Men writhed, bled, and died, for little reason. Valor was spent in butchering the innocent or unlucky.

"We are King Richard's men," said Sir Nigel with a smile that meant, *How can I explain it more clearly than that?* Then he added, "King Richard did not trust his brother. Why should we?"

"If I face further punishment," said Edmund, "I do not wish any of your blood to be spilled." His voice was steady, but he had a distant, frightened look in his eye.

Sir Nigel laughed. "Do you think we have fought together and braved these foul seas to see you captured by the Exchequer's men?"

Edmund could make no direct answer to this. "I sinned by serving a counterfeiter," he said in a low, confiding voice. "I knew my master was cheapening the king's silver—"

Edmund had never opened his heart so freely on this subject. I put a hand on his arm. "When our masters sin, we do, too," I said.

"And we have earned Heaven's forgiveness," said Nigel. "Show me a man perfectly sinless, and I'll show you a creature hard to love."

"Perhaps I deserve further punishment," said Edmund, in that deeply considered way I both admired and found, at times, so exasperating.

"Don't be a fool, Edmund! What is Rannulf here but a murderer?" said Nigel with a laugh. "What am I but a wencher and a drunkard, when Heaven affords me the chance? Besides," Nigel continued, "some devilment is at work here. These officials knew that Edmund was coming home, and they were waiting for him."

"How is that possible?" I asked—although I nearly guessed the truth.

"Hubert," said Nigel with a gentle laugh, "I was once as innocent of the world's spiteful ways as you pretend to be."

"Some slanderer has been at work," I offered.

"Sir Jean himself," said Nigel, "or may Heaven unman me."

I was shaken at the thought of what we faced in London. Then my old habit of spirit returned—hope, that ever flowering shrub. Surely Nigel was mistaken. Surely, I reassured myself, we would not need the swords we strapped on as darkness fell. Rannulf found the ship's armorer, a bald old man with huge hands.

"The sea air will have dulled our steel by now," said Rannulf.

Yet another *fylor* sparked as it put a fresh edge on our swords.

THIRTY·NINE

I could not take a straight step.

The rough planks of the wharf seemed to rise up to meet me, and I stumbled. I had to laugh. Sir Nigel staggered, and only Edmund made anything like a dignified departure from the ship. I was so accustomed to the ceaseless lift and fall of the vessel after months at sea that every step I took was like the lumbering of a drunkard.

Unable to walk upright for the moment, I joined Sir Nigel in prayer, the knight's quiet voice thanking our Lord Jesus Christ, "from whom proceeds all goodness."

Sir Rannulf knelt, either in prayer or to steady himself, and Sir Luke likewise took a few strides and sank, his mantle draped over his shoulders.

I realized as I struggled to my feet that Edmund was hurrying ahead, up toward a dock crowded with barrels, columns of wine casks in the dim torchlight. I realized too late that if there was trouble, Edmund intended to meet it alone and not entangle his friends.

I called out.

A shadow shifted and separated from the stacked drums of wine. Other shadows followed, and these creeping figures were joined by still others, ink pouring down out of the far reaches of the docks, taking shape in the form of the black leather armor of the Exchequer's men.

These assailants closed fast, and I heard a questioning voice. "Are you Edmund, the counterfeiter's apprentice?"

As I ran toward them, I made out the glint of crossbow triggers, and the dimly shining iron points of the crossbow bolts as men shouldered the weapons, aiming them at me.

I could not see Edmund in the tangle of Exchequer's men. I stopped short, breathing hard, five crossbows poised to send their quarrels directly into my head. Rannulf drew his sword and hurried toward the cocked weapons, and I had to block him with my body, begging Rannulf to spare his own life.

Rannulf said nothing, but he did not sheathe his weapon.

"This is an insult to the king," said Sir Luke, falsetto with emotion.

"We are Crusaders!" Sir Nigel exclaimed. "With news of King Richard—and the fall of Acre."

"Sir Nigel and Sir Rannulf are welcome to London," said a smoothed-voiced Exchequer's man, "and the worthy Sir Luke. But we have a warrant for this felon's arrest."

"Show me the seal," said Sir Nigel.

The scroll was handed over, and even in the bad light of

the wharf, it was plain that a heavy portion of wax had been impressed upon the document.

"This is the Exchequer's seal, no doubt," said Sir Nigel, running his fingers over the patch of hard wax, then handing back the warrant. "However, we have a letter of credence from the royal envoy to Rome—the king's personal representative. You will not arrest Squire Edmund."

"We were so commanded," said the Exchequer's man. "New officials have come to London from France, accompanying our lord Prince John. Every outstanding warrant is reissued, and every old crime freshly punished." His voice softened. "I mean no disrespect to good Christian knights, but I follow orders. In any legal matter, we are now Prince John's men."

I could feel a spasm of frustration run through Rannulf as I kept my body between him and the crossbows.

"I know your voice," said Sir Nigel, peering through the poor light at the pale face above the black leather breastplate. "Or one very like it."

"It's possible that Sir Nigel knew my father," said the Exchequer's man in a formal but gentler tone. "A bachelor knight with a head of red hair—"

"Brian de Lynn!" said Nigel. "A knight who could drink ale with me from sunset to sunrise, singing sinner's tales. And you must be young Clifford—Heaven's blessings on you."

"My late father spoke well of you," said Clifford, with the grace to sound embarrassed. "He used to say days like those will never come again."

Sir Luke put a hand on Nigel's shoulder. "If these men have clear orders—"

Rannulf's voice surprised us all, deliberate, unexcited, the words of a man who had made an irrevocable decision. "If you arrest my squire," said the knight, speaking as clearly as his scarred lips allowed, "you arrest me, too."

"And," said Sir Nigel, "all the rest of us as well."

FORTY

Martin de Asterby, the Royal Exchequer, apologized for not standing as we entered his chamber.

"I am not a healthy man," he said.

"It grieves us to hear it, my lord," said Sir Nigel.

"I cough bloody sputum, morning and night," said Martin. "I meet a priest every evening." He was one of the most powerful men in England, and sheriffs and barons alike trembled at the suggestion that the Exchequer felt they had underpaid their taxes. The quality of coinage, and punishment of robbery on the High Way, all fell under his care.

We wore royal livery, with the woolen leopard insignia, freshly brushed, at our breasts. We had spent the preceding night in the Tower of London, a castle of stone built by William the Conqueror and used for various noted guests—envoys and traitors.

Sir Luke had pleaded complicated responsibilities the

night before, and left to carry them out, but the rest of us hushed Edmund's protests, and his expressions of gratitude. Our prison rooms were as comfortable as many chambers I had seen, and we dined on honeyed wine and stewed pears, and mutton that was as tough as any cob-horse, but a treat after shipboard fare.

Now Edmund stood with us—weighed down with chains.

"You are not the first travelers to have tidings of King Richard," said the Exchequer, coughing wetly. He wore a blue tunic of worsted wool, his full sleeves gathered at his wrists. The leopard insignia blazed over his heart, but a smaller emblem than others I had seen. Perhaps Prince John was offended to be reminded that this was still King Richard's London, and no doubt a wise Exchequer sought ways to accommodate a prince. The hilt of a decorative short sword protruded over the edge of the table, its pommel a single brilliant garnet.

"Sir Nicholas de Foss and Sir Jean de Chartres," Martin was saying, "returned nearly a month ago, and filled London with wonder at the tales of King Richard, and the stories of the misdeeds of a certain Crusading squire, a counterfeiter's lad."

Sir Nicholas. So the tall squire had been knighted.

I was not surprised at the further anger the news stirred in me.

Sir Nigel reached within his cloak pocket, and displayed a leather roll with a silver leopard device. He withdrew the letter of credence from its covering.

Martin gave a low, phlegm-choked chuckle at the sight of

this document. "You need no introduction to me. None of you do, all prayerful fighting men in the king's service." He spoke the best Anglo-Frankish, his accent that of a noble-man. "If only I could please every supplicant who came before me," said the Exchequer, "I would die in bliss. Prince John has examined the accounts, and believes his brother's Crusade is costing far too much money."

"What is the price," asked Sir Nigel, "for freeing our companion?"

"Seven hundred gold marks," said the Exchequer.

Sir Nigel protested, with an incredulous laugh, "My lord, the price is too high."

"Are you telling me," asked the Exchequer silkily, "that you returned from the Holy Land with empty purses?"

The service of the finest fighting knight for a year could be purchased for one hundred marks. The price on Ed-mund's freedom was cruel.

"We assert his innocence," said Sir Nigel. Then he added, "Given time, and your lordship's patience, I could pay this fee—"

"How many days," asked Martin, "before you can pay the sum—on your honor?"

Nigel was at a loss for words. "On my honor, I cannot say when I will have so much gold," he said at last, sounding defeated.

"I have testimony against Edmund," said Martin. "I have the evidence of two good Christian men who say that while on Crusade he kept a servant who was trained by himself in the art of thievery."

"The witnesses have lied," said Sir Rannulf.

Martin ran a thoughtful finger over his lips. "An hour with an interrogator will break the truth from his bones. And it has been a good long while since the folk of London have seen a man disemboweled and hanged."

What made me speak just then, my voice ringing out, I shall never guess. "My lord, we assert our privilege to trial by combat."

Trial by combat was the traditional way out of a legal impasse. It was believed that Heaven played a hand in such a contest, favoring the side in the right.

Nigel turned to me and gave me a look the character of which he had never given me before—measuring, nearly respectful.

He did not contradict me.

"Do you?" Martin stifled a cough, and took a sip from a finely wrought silver cup. A servant stepped to his side and poured wine from a pitcher, the beverage spiced with leaves and flecks of stems. Martin gazed into the wine cup, waiting for the medicinal herbs to settle.

"My lord," said Sir Rannulf, "this is our desire, before Heaven."

Martin tasted his medicine. "The two of you, Nigel and Rannulf, joined by—this other young squire—"

"Hubert of Bakewell, my lord," I heard myself say.

"Prince John desires revenue," said Martin with a weary smile. "He does not want to see you kill each other."

"Perhaps," Sir Luke suggested from the back of the chamber, "negotiations might reduce the burden—"

Nigel turned and fixed him with a glance.

Martin's brow smoothed, as though some inner mental

struggle was just now resolved. "I shall not allow Edmund to take up arms in his own defense, you understand. You three will be his champions—is that your wish?"

Nigel spoke for us. "That is our wish, my lord."

"If you intend to fight," Martin continued after a long moment, "the spectacle will please these city folk and members of the royal household who are not able to see the glory of the Crusade. I myself thrill like a boy at the sight of lance and shield. But I will caution you. If those men who champion the squire lose this contest, then Edmund will face the executioner."

"Tomorrow," said Sir Nigel, "we will take up our lances against these perjurers."

"And this young squire, this bright-eyed Hubert," said Martin, "will have to fight like all the rest, lance to lance."

Edmund's chains chimed, the heavy links grating on the oak floor as Edmund strained to catch my eye. I saw him shaking his head at me out of the corner of my vision.

"Good Sir Nigel," added Martin with something close to gentle concern, "do you see how travel-worn you are? You bleed from your gums, the whites of your eyes are yellow, and a month of banqueting might bring you half your usual vigor. If I let this joust go forward as you wish, this capable young Edmund will die."

"We put our lives in God's hands," protested Nigel.

Martin gave a gentle laugh. "I will not survive much longer myself, I'm greatly afraid, and I do not wish the lives of two travel-weakened knights on my soul. Why should two famous Crusading knights such as Nigel and Rannulf die so soon after arriving in England?"

I sensed the words he was about to utter.

"I command this young Hubert to do the fighting," said Martin, "lance to lance, against young Sir Nicholas. Only those two combatants—none other." He leaned forward, and put his elbows on the table. "Or do you wish to deliver a strongbox of gold marks to me by nightfall?"

Nigel was rigid with emotion, his lips quivering as he mentally searched for the argument that would alter the Exchequer's decision.

Martin turned to one of his men. He gave a quiet word, and, chains dragging on the floor, Edmund was led away.

FORTY·ONE

I have never before been in such a stew of feeling, angry and afraid for my friend.

Even after I was taken with Nigel and Rannulf to a noble house, with a courtyard where servants swept paving stones, I could not sit still. I paced about the room, in a whirlpool of troubled humors.

Only after darkness fell and Nigel and Rannulf assembled armor, an assortment of helmets, and a collection of mail suits—my own Crusading mail had grown rigid with rust—did I begin to be afraid for myself.

And then I was nearly speechless.

The two knights enjoyed pullets from the prince's own buttery, brought down to us by a royal steward, a highly placed man-at-arms who bowed and showed every sign of respect for us—especially for me, nodding and smiling in the kindest manner. It was, I recognized too well, the respect people show toward those who will soon be killed.

"I am Elias de Boves," said the steward, a sunny-faced man with bronze curls and a quiet manner. "A man-at-arms, most recently from Aquitaine, where I have been serving the prince."

"I know the village of Boves," said Rannulf. "A storied ogre lived beneath a vineyard there, turning the green grapes black."

"The very place," said Elias.

"Why did the prince break his word?" asked Sir Nigel. "He told his brother he would stay in France until the Crusade's end."

"Who am I," replied Elias, "to question princely matters?"

I was half grateful for such chatter, and half driven mad by it. I wanted to see Father Giles, wherever he might be. I wanted to see my parents and my sister. I wished to speak with Edmund, with Galena—and I wanted to be alone with my thoughts.

"After tomorrow's ordeal," said the steward in a sweetly tempered voice, "my lord Prince John will be pleased to dine with Sir Nigel and Sir Rannulf and hear yet more tidings of his brother the king."

"And with Hubert and Edmund, too," said Nigel pointedly. "You'll want to learn how they fared during the great siege."

The steward's smile broadened. "Of course—my prince will meet with the two squires as well."

———

I did not sleep that night.

Rannulf and Nigel sat up with me, reciting the ballads every Christian fighting man loves, the stories of swords found embedded in hoary oaks; of Our Lady appearing before millers and sheriff's deputies and other such notorious sinners, and changing their lives.

Of Daniel in the pit filled with lions, afraid to move, afraid to stand still, until he was afraid of nothing.

FORTY·TWO

The rooks woke early the next morning.

"A happy omen," said Nigel, regarding their common-place, merry bickering, "if ever I heard one."

As I spoke to the servants, I sounded, in my own ears, like a knight who had been through years of battle and cared little whether he faced one more contest. It was very nearly how I felt. Having been angry and terrified, now I wanted only for the day to be done. The servants of the house brought in ewers of hot water, as I requested. I bathed in a fine copper tub, and Nigel scrubbed my back.

I donned a shirt of linen, freshly laundered by Rannulf and dried before the fire. I wore a Crusader tunic, marked with a white cross, also carefully tended by Rannulf. My surcoat of rich blue, with the leopard triumphant, was prepared by Nigel, working with a fine brush in the early-morning light.

184

Helmet padding, leg wraps, woolen gloves—one by one I put on the inner garments of my armor. Then Nigel held up the heavy body mail, the veteran knight acting as my squire on this spring morning. Worked down over my head, the mail skirt hung full, all the way to my ankles, the familiar but half-forgotten weight almost succeeding in preparing me for what I was going to do that day. I would wear an iron jousting helmet, like a great bucket, with a grill for vision and breath. This armor would afford me better protection by far than the modest squire helmet I had worn in Chios.

"Where is Edmund?" I asked.

"He spent the night in the Tower," said Rannulf, "and I am told that he is well."

"When will I see him?"

Neither knight would answer, but at last Nigel said, "He'll be there."

Edmund is stronger than I am. I did not utter the thought, or complete it in my own mind—that Edmund would succeed in a joust where I might fail.

Perhaps Nigel read the thought in my eyes. "Edmund has never couched a lance under his arm," he said in a quiet, matter-of-fact tone, "and remember, Hubert—no one's blade is quicker than yours."

My sword was polished by Rannulf, worked over with goat-bone marrow until the steel was bright.

Then we went down to the riverbank and crossed the Thames on a ferry—the Church had forbidden even legal jousts within the city walls.

185

FORTY-THREE

The field was green, and the verges were bright with the yellow flower folk in Bakewell call the daffadown, and others name the daffodil, the flowers stretching up a far-off hillside to a stand of leafless trees. It was perhaps the first warm day of spring, one of the days when the sky is huge and the sun close. Beyond was the city and the Tower.

Prince John looked very little like his brother. While King Richard was a yellow-haired, thick-necked bull of a man, his brother was lean and dark-haired, and he did not trouble wearing even a decorative sword. He sat protected from the noon sun by a canopy high above the grass, toying with the topaz ring on his finger. He offered a remark to Martin the Exchequer, who perched beside him, heavily muffled in a cloak. Martin laughed politely. Surrounding the prince was a group of household knights, each armed with a sword and *couteau*.

For myself, I felt duty toward the king, and the proper respect for the prince. I felt little love for either.

Nearby, accompanied by spearmen, stood Edmund, the iron shackles gleaming on his wrists. His eyes met mine, and his lips shaped words—some heartfelt prayer, I was certain. The chain smith attended him, to strike the chains free or to bind him further, however the day unfolded.

On both sides of the tourney field was a swarm of people. Many were drinking, celebrating by gesturing and acting out battle, showing each other how they would wield a sword if they were fighting this day. I recognized sailors from the *Saint Susanna,* and Captain Hawkmoor caught my eye, lifting both hands before him prayerfully, offering a faithful smile. Many men were armed with staves, and I knew exactly the sort of melee that could result if the crowd grew angry. Banners and flags tossed in the light breeze, and somewhere a pie man called, "Hot, plenty and hot."

My mount was a ten-year-old warhorse called Oak-heart, provided by the king's own ostler. He was described as too old for war, but still in his prime for jousting, where big bones and an appetite for fighting favors the experienced steed. As is usual for a joust, I wore a spur only on my left heel, a knob of polished iron.

Sir Nicholas's silken, heavily muscled charger flared his nostrils and foamed at the bit. The newly dubbed knight's surcoat displayed the fighting symbol of his former master, the golden swift with its graceful wing cocked in flight. When I rode across the field to offer my respects in the highest speech I could muster, I looked into his eyes as though to share some query with him.

"A good day to you, squire," he said in response, both to my spoken and unspoken communication. He was the same sun-freckled, good-sized young man as before, but with an increased air of dignity.

I felt again that under some other stars, in another year, Nicholas and I might have shared ale together and swapped dreams of glory. Now I recalled being carried bodily by my companions, and long nights with a throbbing head.

But I did not feel anger.

I had seen it in Edmund, too, how this stride and gesture, even his voice, had taken on the weight and bearing of a fighting man.

I raised the hilt of the sword to my lips, as is the proper thing, and kissed it.

The master of the tournament, dressed in fine yellow stockings and a green doublet, explained that this was no game-joust, but a battle to the death. There would be no rest periods for the winded or momentarily stunned, and none of the rules that made jousting fair and—for some—pleasurable. Any blow or tactic fit for a battlefield would be allowed here. The master had something of Fulke's prideful bearing, a man of intelligence required to look on during the triumphs and defeats of other souls.

Some protocol apparently required that each of us acknowledge the mortality we both faced, because Sir Nicholas sat beside me on his restless mount and announced for all to hear, "I forgive any who may this day do me any harm." The joust in Chios had been a mere game, I knew, a tournament for pride and rough sport, compared with the legal manslaughter about to take place.

The master looked to me expectantly. I felt the weight of the sword at my hip as I forgave whoever might take my life.

FORTY·FOUR

Then the master of the tournament knelt before the prince.

The prince smiled and made some quiet remark, and the master rose and clapped his hands gently together, a signal to his clerks.

He was brought a sword from which hung a heavy cloth of woven dimity. Such stout signal cloths were often used in tourneys, lest an errant breeze flutter a light linen flag prematurely to the ground. The ladies in the crowd adjusted their hoods, the men set their caps squarely on their heads, each observer bracing for whatever was to follow.

The men-at-arms wore swords and gauntlets—if this joust became a general battle, they were ready. Square-jawed Sir Jean himself sat astride a charger, a lance held upright. Sir Rannulf, too, had brought a mount onto the field, although he stood beside it. When I caught his eye, the knight lifted a mailed fist of encouragement. I wondered if my under-standing would ever be equal to the stony, complex nature of that scarred man-at-arms. Sir Nigel was in bright chain mail, as erect as a man ready to recite every Psalm. And it was true as I looked at them in this sunlight—the two knights did look weathered and worn.

The master of the tournament took a few steps, maintaining his control over us as our chargers tossed their heads. The master had a fixed smile, neither good-humored nor encouraging, and many in the crowd kept their hands folded tight, praying or questioning their wagers. No voice cheered or mocked us. The crowd grew silent.

With an expert flick of the master's wrist, the cloth plummeted without a flutter to the ground.

I couched the lance under my elbow as I had been trained, and balanced it against the rocking of my mount, my body held tightly in place by the padded vise of the saddle. Sir Nicholas spurred his charger, rocking to one side to confuse me or to improve the angle of his attack.

Like any jousting knight, I wore my buckler on a strap around my neck, but the shield proved of little immediate use. Sir Nicholas's lance struck my saddle in the breastplate, jolting the horse badly as the weapon broke in two, splinters flying. Sir Nicholas, an enigmatic figure in his dark, gleaming helmet, swayed in his saddle, his rein hand flailing involuntarily as my own lance caught his surcoat half a heartbeat later, tearing it, passing close to the young knight's body.

As he lurched by, he deliberately dragged the jagged remnant of his lance across my helmet, the broken wood ringing off the iron. The blow half deafened me, and I worked to position the helmet squarely over my head again. I reeled to the end of the field and turned my mount.

Oak-heart inhaled and exhaled heavily, the heat of the big charger rising up and enveloping me. I was breathing hard, too, and I had the unreal impression that events were moving too quickly, that I was still soaking my morning bread in sweet wine, or testing the edge of my sword against a blade of grass.

A new lance was brought out and pressed into Nicholas's grasp.

Then, without further delay, my opponent's lance was leveled, and he approached speedily, the brilliant iron point directed right at my chest. I had barely begun my charge, and the momentum was all his. He was already too close for me to do any more than steady my lance and brace myself. The two of us collided, the force slamming the breath from my body. Our weapons fell from our hands, and I reached out and seized Nicholas's helmet as he struggled to get by me.

Our two horses joined in the fight, forced into each other. Nicholas's horse bit into mine, the horses' necks locking, the animals screaming as they rose on their hind legs, struggled, fell.

Oak-heart rolled on me, and my leg went numb. Nicholas was on his feet at once, his crimson surcoat bunched, torn at one shoulder, his sword in hand. I staggered to my feet, dragging my leg, and working my hand through the straps in my shield. Nicholas and I both had to dance clumsily away from our horses as they climbed back onto their feet, sweating, spiked with crushed turf. Nicholas stabbed at me, holding his sword two-handed, an efficient and deadly lunge, except that I fell back.

Stunned, confused, I had neglected to draw my sword, blocking my opponent's blade with my buckler. I tugged my weapon from its sheathe and at once struck Nicholas in the head, my blade biting into the iron basin of his helmet, but unable to cut through the smith-toughened metal.

The knight staggered, reached out for the reins of his steed, clinging briefly to his mount for support. Through the crosshatch slits in his iron armor, his eyes searched momentarily for his companions, standing at the side of the field.

I struck Nicholas in the shoulder, the hacking blow cutting through the chain mail. My opponent's sword arm went slack, and his weapon dropped. It was impossible to see the blood against the crimson surcoat, but the fabric gleamed wetly. His horse panicked, backing away, Nicholas struggling to stay upright, bright blood gushing through the rent in his mail. I struck him again, bones snapping.

The young knight slipped, almost gracefully, to the trampled grass. He knelt there, helmeted head to the turf, his crimson surcoat sodden, and then rolled to one side like a boneless thing, all but lifeless. I had time to feel only a brief anguish at the sight, a flicker of pity and relief.

The sounds from the world were muted by my armor and the wool helmet pad, but even so I could hear the rush of intaken breath in one hundred lungs as something happened, some new event caught the crowd. I turned to face whatever it was.

Sir Jean was riding hard, kicking his charger, the point of his lance aimed steadily at me.

FORTY·FIVE

I had just enough agility and strength to cause the point to miss, crouching and blocking the weapon with my shield, but the weight of the jousting lance was punishing, pressing me down as it passed.

I sought Sir Jean with the point of my sword, spinning and lunging as he thundered by. The heat of his charger captured me, foam and horse sweat spattering my armor as I angled upward with the sword, finding him, driving deep into flesh and bone. He struck me, and struck me again with the butt of his lance, the crashing blows numbing me through the iron.

He fell on me, and knocked me down. We both swayed to our feet. I had a dim, gray vision of my sword belaboring the big knight, and my opponent seizing his own blade and striking marrow-stunning blows in return, bruising my shield arm, punishing my helmet. Blood or mucus streamed from my nose, and my knees buckled under every blow.

But I did not go down again.

And I fought. When I stepped forward, each time, my grip aching as I swung my sword, Sir Jean took a step back, too, unable to stand his ground, blood gleaming on his dark gauntlets.

We battled like that for long moments, my lungs on fire, my sword arm losing all sensation as Sir Jean retreated raggedly, staggering. At last we both collapsed, and for a few heartbeats I did not move.

With no warning Sir Rannulf was there, tugging Sir Jean's helmet free. Rannulf stood over Sir Jean, gasping as much as he could of "Yield your sword, by Jesu." Tears of relief streamed down his face as he saw me sit up and begin to make an effort to stand once more.

Sir Jean attempted to speak, but he could make no sound. He mouthed, "I yield."

Rannulf knelt to cut his throat, but I swung to my feet and fell upon Rannulf, wresting the knife from his hand.

For a long, suffocating moment I tried to tug my helmet free, half deaf and breathing hard, but there was no strength in my hands. I could only see the shape of my name on Edmund's lips as he ran toward me, leaping, free.